THE SEASHELL
OF 'Ohana

Other Books by Mary Ting

Adult – Clean Romance
Spirit of Ohana Series
When the Wind Chimes, Book 1

Young Adult
International Sensory Assassin Network Series
ISAN, Book 1
HELIX, Book 2
GENES, Book 3
CODE, Book 4

Forthcoming from Mary Ting

International Sensory Assassin Network Series
AVA, Book 5

Awards

Spirit of 'Ohana Series
Grand Prize Winner: Romantic Fiction, Chatelaine Book Awards
Gold Medal: Romance, Kops-Fetherling International Book Awards
Gold Medal: Romance, New York Book Festival
Bronze Medal: Romance, Independent Publisher Book Awards (IPPY)
Finalist: Romance, Next Generation Indie Book Awards

International Sensory Assassin Network Series
Gold Medal: Science Fiction & Fantasy, Benjamin Franklin Awards
Gold Medal: Science Fiction—Post-Apocalyptic, American Fiction Awards
Gold Medal: Science Fiction, International Book Awards
Gold Medal: Young Adult Thriller, Readers' Favorite Awards
Gold Medal: Young Adult Action, Readers' Favorite Awards
Silver Medal: YA Fantasy / Sci-Fi, Moonbeam Children's Book Awards
Finalist: Action Adventure, Silver Falchion Awards

Jaclyn and the Beanstalk
Bronze Medal: Juvenile / YA Fiction, Illumination Book Awards
Finalist: YA Mythology / Fairy Tale, Readers' Favorite Book Awards
Finalist: Young Adult Fiction, Best Book Awards
Finalist: Unpublished Manuscript, Hollywood Book Festival

THE SEASHELL
OF 'Ohana

Spirit of 'Ohana, Book 2

MARY TING

The Seashell of 'Ohana

This is a work of fiction. Names, characters, places, and incidents either are the product of the author's imagination or are used fictitiously.
Any resemblance to actual persons, living or dead, or locales is entirely coincidental.

Cover design by Michael J. Canales
www.MJCImageworks.com

ISBN: 978-1-64548-086-0

Published by Rosewind Books
An imprint of Vesuvian Books
www.RosewindBooks.com

Printed in the United States

10 9 8 7 6 5 4 3 2 1

Table of Contents

Chapter One — Lucky Day

The wheels on our shopping cart squeaked across the tile floor, drawing annoyed glances from other shoppers. Of all the carts, we got this one.

Tyler didn't seem to mind the persistent squeak, so I left it alone. My son walked ahead, pushing the cart without me.

The young cashier smiled as he passed. Her eyes met mine. "Hi, Abby."

I nodded in return. The slightly frayed hem of Tyler's pants brushed the top of his ankles. He needed a new pair of jeans. When had he outgrown them?

"Ty, not too fast." I speed-walked behind him, my arms outstretched, ready to take the reins.

Tyler glared over his shoulder, squinting his brown eyes at me with an obvious "don't tell me what to do" look.

He'd turned eight recently and had been testing boundaries by talking back to me, asking to play video games before he did his homework, or staying up later during the school nights.

Being a single mom was hard enough, but it wore my patience thin when he fought me at every step. I narrowed my eyes at him, even though he had turned back and couldn't see me. At least he had slowed down.

Next to a paper towel sale display, a woman pulled her toddler to the side. She lowered her gaze to the wheels on our cart and frowned at the noise. She had enough room, but you couldn't be too careful with toddlers. I would have done the same.

"Sorry." I offered an affable smile with a wave.

My black flats slapped with the rhythm of his steps. I wasn't an overbearing parent, but Tyler had rammed our cart into a grumpy old woman last week.

We didn't need another accident.

Thank God the old woman hadn't been injured. But even after Tyler had apologized, she'd flipped us off. Tyler had had the shock of his life, then I'd had the shock of mine when my son let out a belly laugh and pointed at her. The laugh had been so loud that it had seized everyone's attention. I had been mortified, beyond humiliated, but at the same time, an inappropriate giggle had bubbled up my throat.

I'd grabbed my son and the cart and booked it out of the vegetable section before the old lady could throw more profanity at us. I hoped I didn't run into her today, or any other day, for that matter.

All the cashiers knew us, as I had shopped at this grocery store at least once a week for the past four years—our little community market in Poipu, Kauai. After my husband passed away, Tyler and I moved to Kauai to heal.

Squeak, squeak, squeak.

Tyler veered the cart to the bread aisle. He slowed to squeeze past a middle-aged man who had his cart smack in the middle of the lane. I had a routine, and Tyler knew exactly where to go.

"Do we need hamburger buns, Mom?"

"No, not today. Follow me." I adjusted my purse strap over my shoulder and strode past the canned vegetables and soups, repeating my short list under my breath. *Cereal. Eggs. Yogurt. Butter lettuce.*

I had written down what I needed but had forgotten to bring the list, having left it inside the cup holder in my minivan. *Ugh!* I should text it to myself next time. No matter, I only needed four things.

Cereal. Eggs. Yogurt. Butter lettuce. More than once, I'd gone to the market and walked out without the item I'd intended to buy in the first place.

"This way, Ty." I turned into the cereal aisle but halted, distracted by the scent of something sweet.

Fresh leis made with pink and purple orchids and plumeria hung on a small rack at the floral section. Big balloons read "Happy Birthday" and "I love you," alongside bouquets of various flowers. Steve used to buy me flowers.

Plumeria was one of my local favorites, and I loved how they smelled like ripe peaches. I had some in a water bowl in my house that I had picked from the tree in my front yard. I smiled, imagining the flowers Steve would bring home if he'd lived.

My reverie dissolved when a pale woman twirled the revolving shelves with Kauai magnets near the flower section. A guy with heavy black glasses showed her a Kauai T-shirt he'd grabbed from the near shelf. They must be tourists.

"Mom, can I buy this one?" Tyler handed me a box, his eyes gleaming.

I examined the ingredients on the back. Organic. Low fat. Low sugar. Hardly any sodium. Even had calcium and fiber. *Good.* But Tyler liked the chocolate flavor, and this was vanilla. I saw why he wanted it when I flipped it to the front.

The cereal bits were shaped like skulls and pirate hats. His favorite video game used to be *Unicorns versus Skeletons*, but he had outgrown it and advanced to *Buccaneers versus Skeletons*. A small plastic figure of one of the characters came inside the box.

I leveled my eyes to his. "Are you going to eat it?"

When my younger sister Kate was little, she used to beg our mother to buy certain cereals just for the toy. My mother had always given in, and of course, Kate had never finished the box. As I contemplated buying it, I wondered if I would eat the cereal.

"Aye, Captain. I promise." Tyler slung his arm like a pirate and placed a hand over his heart on his T-shirt.

"Are you *sure*?" I lowered my eyebrows. I wasn't going to let him get away with it if he didn't. A promise was a promise—a word he shouldn't use lightly to get his way.

Tyler pinched his eyebrows together and paused as if in thought. He grabbed the box, shelved it, and took out a smaller one of the same kind.

"This one is on sale, and it comes with the same toy," he said. "If I don't finish it, then you can take it out of my allowance."

I resisted hugging him in public, but I was so proud. What eight-year-old would say such a thing? It had been just Tyler and me for almost four years without Steve. He'd had to grow up faster than most kids his age, including learning about finances earlier than I'd anticipated.

"Well, since you put it that way, and you've obviously learned the skill of negotiation, I'll take that deal." I placed the box in the cart.

"Shiver me timbers." Tyler's face glowed with happiness, his lips curling upward.

I shook my head, smiling. With those glowing brown eyes, that sharp nose, and the grin spreading to his ears, he looked so much like his father. The dagger that lived in my heart stabbed a little deeper.

Cereal. Scratch that off the list. *Eggs, yogurt, and butter lettuce.*

Squeak, squeak, squeak went the wheels as Tyler trailed behind me. The noise sounded louder in the deserted milk and egg section.

I grabbed a carton of jumbo brown eggs and strolled to the next refrigerated section near the butcher. While Tyler busied himself by looking at the cereal box, I placed my purse inside the cart and reached for the yogurt. The brand Tyler and I liked was on the top and pushed all the way back.

I got on my tiptoes and pressed my body closer as I stretched my arm up, but I still couldn't grab it. Didn't they know some shoppers were petite? I let out a groan, gave a little hop, and landed with a clomp. Almost, but I wasn't going to be able to reach it no matter how many times I leaped.

I cursed under my breath and glanced to either side. No workers. None of the few customers passing by appeared tall enough to help. I certainly wasn't going to ask the old woman slowly strolling by, who was scrutinizing me like I was going to steal something.

With no other choice, I stepped on a small ledge, about two feet high, and then pushed upward. *Got one. Success.* But my smile was quickly replaced with panic. My foot slipped on the metal, and I teetered, trying to right myself even as I knew it was a losing battle. I twisted on my way down, about to fall flat on my face.

Thoughts flashed through my mind. Tyler was going to be without a mom, or I would break a limb, leaving us both helpless.

This had been a reckless, asinine decision. How many times had I scolded Tyler for jumping on his bed? How often had I emphasized that he could crack his skull or break a leg if he slipped and landed on the floor wrong?

As I prepared for the fall, I threw up a quick prayer.

Footsteps pounded, and then my back collided with something firm. I let out an oomph and was enveloped by a wave of musky scent mixed with ocean breeze.

Oh, thank God.

I knew that scent. I hadn't forgotten even after all these years. But it couldn't be him. My breath caught. Two strong arms helped me to a standing position, and I met the familiar gorgeous brown eyes sparkling with shock and recognition. My heart skipped pleasantly at the sight of Ian Bordonaro.

"Are you okay?"

His smooth, deep voice sent all sorts of unwanted tingles through my veins. *Does he even remember who I am?* "Thanks for the rescue. I'm Abby Fuller."

An amused grin lit his face. "I remember you, Abby."

Ian wore dark jeans and a black T-shirt, and this simple attire combined with his five o'clock shadow had me thinking things I shouldn't.

THE SEASHELL OF 'OHANA

It had been about three years since I'd seen him, but I hadn't forgotten his scent, his sexy deep voice, or that handsome face. He'd appeared like a hot guardian angel just when I needed him.

Stop thinking about hot angels in fantasy books.

"Ty. It's nice to see you." Ian went straight for Tyler. "You've grown taller. How are you?"

"Hi, Ian. How are you?" Tyler held the cereal box with the other arm as they shook hands.

I was surprised Tyler recognized Ian and proud that he'd remembered his manners. My lectures had paid off—twice in one day.

Ian's grin widened. "Good. Thanks for asking. So, you're helping your mom."

"Yeah, sort of." Tyler lowered his voice, his shoulders drooping a little. "I had no choice. Mom forgot a few things from the market, again." He said the last word with a pained sigh.

Ian let out a chuckle, and that sound reached something inside me. He gave me a once-over like he was checking me out. My cheeks warmed, and I suddenly forgot how to breathe.

I was sure I had bags under my eyes, and my long hair was a tangled mess. I'd had a rough day at the art gallery and had rushed over here. I hadn't met with clients today, so I had on an old pair of gray jeans and a white T-shirt, purple and yellow oil paint staining the hem.

A pause stretched between us. A few women passed, their eyes on Ian, admiring him a bit too long. He didn't notice as his attention was on me. I couldn't remember the last time I felt so ... *seen*.

"Pure. That's my favorite." Ian pointed at my hand, breaking the silence.

Apparently, I had forgotten what I was doing here. "Oh, yes. Pure is our favorite, too."

"Do you need just one?" He let out the same delicious chuckle and made me want to hear him laugh again.

I gave him a sidelong glance. "Just one ...?"

"Yogurt?" He sounded unsure.

"Oh, this." I raised the yogurt. "Yes. I mean, no." I shook my head. *Stop acting like a girl with a crush.* "I mean, I need a few more. Could you, please?"

His toned biceps flexed as he grabbed a container and placed it in the cart. My gaze lingered over his thick eyebrows framing deep-set dark eyes with killer eyelashes that gave the illusion he was wearing eyeliner. He reminded me of the hot pirate character in Tyler's game.

He halted as he stretched his arm to grab another container, craned his neck to me, and slowly tugged his lips into a devilish grin. His eyes beamed with amusement that said—*I know you're looking at me.*

I backed away a step with a nervous smile, noticing that my treacherous body had leaned toward him. He placed the one he held gently in the cart on top of two piles he had made by my purse.

"Will ten be enough, or do you need more?" he asked.

Ten? What? I had been too enthralled and hadn't noticed.

"This is plenty. Thank you." I offered a grateful smile and tucked a lock of hair behind my ear. "Were you passing by? I mean, I didn't see you."

I lowered my eyes to the black plastic basket next to his feet. That must have been the thing that had clattered on the ground before he'd caught me. Inside, he had a loaf of wheat bread, two tomatoes in a clear plastic bag, and turkey sandwich meat.

Ian rubbed at his stubbled jaw and flicked his gaze to Tyler. "I was on my way to get some ice cream when I heard a squeaking sound, and I wanted to know who the cart belonged to."

Perhaps lucky after all.

"So, are you back from a business trip?" I asked. "Or are you off to another country?"

I wasn't trying to pry in his personal business, but it'd be weird to thank him and walk off. After all, he was Leonardo's good friend. They were practically brothers. And it wasn't like we were strangers.

Ian grabbed a couple of Pure yogurts and lowered them into his basket. "I got back from Singapore last night. I'll be staying for a while."

I nodded, and an awkward silence fell between us. I put my hand on the cart's handle, about to tell him goodbye, but he said, "Will you be at your gallery any time soon?"

"I'm swamped at work, so I'm there every day."

Ian picked up his basket with one swift scoop. "I need to buy some paintings, so I'll stop by when I get a chance. Anyway, I better let you two get going." He glanced at Tyler, who was shaking the box of cereal near his ear like a Christmas present.

"Thank you for rescuing me." My cheeks heated. "See you around." *See you around?* So lame. I wished I had a redo.

"I'd like that," he said, then gave his attention to Tyler. "Take care of your mom. And …" He leaned lower, but gave me a sly sidelong glance as if he was saying it to me. "Don't forget to buy chocolate chip ice cream. That's my favorite."

"Mine too." Tyler's eyes rounded.

Ian nodded at the box Tyler held, then held out his palm for a high five. "See you soon, kid. Ahoy, mate."

"Blimey." Tyler's smile stretched wider, and he looked at Ian as if he was his hero.

I started when Ian swooped his arms around my waist and placed a tender kiss on my cheek.

"It was good seeing you, Abby." His kind words caressed the shell of my ear.

Ian's warm body was firm against mine, and his stubble lightly grazed my skin. I sucked in a breath, surprised as those touches traveled to places they shouldn't, caressing me like a gentle ocean wave. It happened so fast—it almost felt like it hadn't happened at all.

Scorching heat rose up my neck, and my tongue knotted. He walked away like a surfer riding the wave to the perfect sunset, leaving me pining for another glimpse. Even the refrigerated air of the dairy section couldn't douse the flame burning inside me.

I shivered and came back to myself, but just as I turned, Ian looked back with a heartfelt grin, lightly swinging his basket, and then winked. He walked backward, one step at a time, and grabbed a container of eggs, never taking his eyes off me. Our eyes stayed locked, and my smile might have stretched too wide.

The universe seemed to have stopped rotating. Gone were the sounds of the wheels on the carts rolling by, shoes scuffing against the tile floor, the beep and hum of the cash registers, and the butcher talking to the impatient customers nearby.

"Mom. Mom. Yo ho ho." Someone tugged my shirt. "Can we *please* go now?"

Oh, right. My son.

"Ty. I'm so sorry." I stroked his hair. "Yes, sweetheart. I need to get the butter lettuce, and then we're done."

I didn't look back to see if Ian was still there, but how badly I wanted to. Guilt hit me hard in the pit of my stomach. Guilt for forgetting my dead husband long enough to notice Ian, even only for a few seconds. And Tyler was my focus and would stay that way.

No time for a man in my life. Tyler was my love, my world.

Chapter Two — Welcome Home

T he doorbell chimed, and I leaned over to peer out the kitchen window. Korean barbecue sauce's sweet and spicy aroma filled the house, overpowering the scent of ripe peaches from the plumeria blossoms floating inside the glass bowl on the entry table.

My seashell collection—Puka, cowry, cone, and sunrise shells in delicate colors and patterns—was scattered on the table around the bowl. Tyler and I had collected them from local beaches over the years.

"They're here," Tyler exclaimed.

He bumped the corner of the end table on his way to the door, his bare feet pounding across the wooden floor. A photo of Tyler, Steve, and I rattled and nearly fell over.

"Ty, slow down." I shook my head. That boy had too much energy and not enough caution.

"Ahoy, matey." Tyler and Bridget greeted each other.

I'd misjudged the Friday traffic, so it was a good thing I'd left work early to have ample time to cook. After turning off the oven, I rushed out to usher the guests into my cozy, single-story home.

My sister Kate, her boyfriend Leonardo—Lee to his close friends— and his niece Bridget, who also recently turned eight, wrapped their arms around me in a tight squeeze, one at a time. Kate and Lee had just returned from a vacation while Bridget's nanny had looked after her.

It had only been two weeks, but I was used to seeing my sister every day at the gallery, where we painted side by side. It had kind of gotten lonely without her.

Unlike some sisters, Kate and I were the best of friends. We'd each had friends of our own, but when it came down to it, I trusted no one but her with my secrets and dreams. We'd even gone to the same university and gotten degrees in illustration.

Kate and Lee looked refreshed, their eyes bright and their skin sun-kissed. Bridget went to the living room area with Tyler to play *Buccaneers versus Skeletons* on their tablets. Her braided blonde hair bounced with every step. Lee had adopted Bridget after her mom, his younger sister, had passed away with cancer.

Lee handed me a white box from the local bakery. Swirls of frosting enticed me through the clear plastic lid. "You know I love their desserts."

Lee's dark hair, sleeked back, reminded me of Ian. I blinked to clear the memory of Ian walking away with that understated swagger at the market.

"I'll take that for you." Kate grabbed the dessert box and carried it to the kitchen. She smelled of lilies. It must be a new perfume.

"What are you cooking? It smells good." Lee took off his sneakers and set them on the shoe rack.

"One of your favorites, Lee," I sang.

"Korean beef short ribs?" His brown eyes lit up. Then he tilted his head at my large crystal bowl. "I don't know what smells better—the plumerias or the ribs."

I smiled and patted the back of the sofa. "Have a seat and make yourselves comfortable. I'm almost done cooking." I rushed back to the kitchen.

Kate had nestled the dessert box on the white granite counter by my cell phone and grabbed a pair of red silicone mitts out of the drawer.

"Let me help you." She walked over to the oven. "Are these done?"

Some people fried Korean short ribs on the stove, but I liked to broil them, a trick I'd learned from my mother. They cooked faster and tasted better. Barbecuing was always best, but I didn't have time.

"They're ready. You can take them out." I set the platter of butter lettuce salad, a plate of broccoli, and rice bowls on the dining table. "Ty, Bridget, dinner is ready."

"Coming," they both said.

Footsteps padded behind me as I walked back to Kate. "So, tell me about your vacation."

"After I'm fed." Kate snorted and waved at the smoke from the open oven. She took out the baking sheet and carefully placed the ribs on the large white platter with a pair of tongs.

I poured three glasses of red wine, passed two to Lee and Kate, then eased into a chair in front of my sister.

"I'm feeding you. Are you going to tell me now?" I asked with a hint of sarcasm.

Kate cackled and wrung strands of brunette hair over her ear. She shared a loving glance with Lee and said, "It was amazing. We had the best time."

A romantic getaway. I had no doubt Lee had gone all out in Paris and Rome. When Kate and I had time together, she would spill all, but for now, she was holding back.

"Maybe next time we can all go together," Lee added as he took a bite of the beef. "Yum, Abby. I don't know what you put in the sauce, but I have not tasted anything better than the one you make."

"You're just saying that. You don't have to flatter me." I ducked my head and poured the miso dressing over my salad.

Lee's chest bobbed from his full belly chuckle. "Fine, but it's still the best." His attention shifted to Kate. "Do you want another galbi, babe?"

Kate was already eating one, but he went out of his way to place another on her plate. She rewarded him with a sunshine smile, her brown eyes twinkling, reminding me of our mother.

Kate and I looked similar and yet different. We both had our father's eyes and our mother's smooth, pale skin. I'd gotten my father's nose and full lips. And Kate inherited our mother's narrow jawline.

Lee was always looking after Kate, doting on her and showing love in those small but tangible ways. His actions showed how much he cared for her. As much as I loved seeing that affection between them, it made me miss Steve even more.

Steve had worked long hours and on the weekends, too. And any time he could spare, he'd spent with Tyler and me. Even when his coworkers wanted him to go out for drinks, he had always come home. He had been a wonderful husband and father.

"Mom, I don't want broccoli," Tyler whined, and dumped the few pieces that were on his plate onto mine. He had told me he didn't like broccoli countless times, but I never stopped trying.

I frowned. "Take one bite, Ty."

"Nay, Captain." He wrinkled his nose.

"You're not a pirate." I scowled. "Pirate talk won't get you out of listening to your mother."

"So …" Lee licked the sauce off his fingers. "Anything new happen while we were gone?"

My face got even hotter. Every time I thought of Ian, my whole body ignited. Had Ian told Lee he had bumped into me? Actually saved me from making a fool out of myself and possibly from breaking a bone or two?

I was reluctant to bring it up, but they would definitely meet, since Ian was back in town. He was bound to tell Lee if he hadn't already. And then there was the fact that Tyler was looking at me, waiting for me to speak first. Because I knew he was dying to say something.

"Ty, you want to tell Lee who we ran into yesterday?" I gathered the cool wine glass and took a sip.

"Who, Ty?" Bridget's blue eyes gleamed, reminding me of the ocean.

Tyler swallowed a spoonful of rice, but when his eyes sparkled with mischief, I almost stopped him. But why? There wasn't anything to hide.

"We saw Ian at the market," Ty began. He spoke so fast, I didn't have a chance to cut him off. "He caught my mom like a hero just before she fell. She was trying to get the yogurt, but she was too short. She said a lot of bad words. Mom acted shy, and then they just looked at each other for a while, and I was so bored. Ian said he would see Mom at the gallery. And then he kissed her."

Kate slapped her hand over her mouth, almost spitting out her wine. Lee dipped his head, pretending to be busy with his napkin on his lap. Bridget giggled.

Mortified. Blood drained from my face. My muscles went slack and weak. It was a good thing I was sitting.

Tyler had had his eyes glued on the cereal box when I was talking to Ian. It hadn't seemed like he was paying attention, but he observed more than I knew. More than I wished, sometimes. I had to be careful around him.

I'm a terrible mother.

"Kids say the silliest things. What Tyler was trying to say …" I let out a nervous laugh and stroked Tyler's hair. "Yes, we saw Ian. And yes, he did prevent me from a fall. It was a good thing he was there because I might have broken something. That would have been horrible." I fiddled with a napkin. "Anyway, he just got back from a business trip in Singapore, and he's planning to stop by the gallery because he needed some paintings. And then he kissed my cheek to say goodbye. That's all."

My voice was a little too casual, but it didn't matter anyway. Kate was sure to spot my flaming cheeks. I could try to blame it on the wine, but I had taken only a few sips.

Kate raised an eyebrow, but smiled. That eyebrow promised she'd bombard me with questions as soon as she had the chance.

"Anyway, anyone want more beef?" I asked.

When no one answered, I steered the conversation to the kids' school and upcoming events. After dinner, everyone helped clean up, and then we settled in the family room.

Kate and I served hot jasmine tea and slices of strawberry cake on pretty plates, hand-painted with lavender Hawaiian hibiscus that nearly matched Kate's cute, short-sleeved shirt with ruffles down the buttons. She'd given me the plates last Christmas.

"Yum. This cake is the best." Bridget licked a smear of white buttercream frosting off her bottom lip and shared a laugh with Tyler.

They sat side by side on the hardwood floor by the fireplace, underneath the painting of a sun-soaked beach scene and a tropical mountain with a misty waterfall.

Tyler scooped up a whole forkful of only frosting. "Oh, Mom. Don't forget Jace's birthday party tomorrow."

Jace, Bridget, and Tyler had been friends since preschool.

"I haven't forgotten since the last time you reminded me today," I said.

"Would you like for me to take Tyler so he and Bridget can ride together?" my sister asked.

"I'm good. Thanks, though." Call me clingy, but I was delighted to perform mother duties unless I was busy at work. Grief had taught me to appreciate the little things.

"I have to say," Lee said, "this is the best cake I've ever tasted. The frosting melts in your mouth, and the cake is so soft. I've been missing out for years."

"That's true. You *were* missing out until you met me," Kate said with a wink. "But you can stop flattering us. You've traveled all over the world. Surely you've had better."

Lee kissed Kate's forehead. "It's better because I'm sharing it with you."

Kate's cheeks turned as pink as my shirt. I smiled at their exchange while the kids were in their conversation.

"Anyway ..." Kate placed her plate on the tea table and scampered to the door. She came back with gift bags. "We got something for you and Ty."

"For me?" Tyler dropped his fork with a clank.

I took a sip of the hot jasmine green tea and leaned back into the sofa. "You didn't have to do that. You're supposed to enjoy your time together and not shop for us."

"Lee likes to shop. It's the only reason I keep him around." Kate snorted and handed Tyler and me each a bag.

I parted the tissue paper and pulled out a scarf printed with Claude Monet's *White Water-Lilies*.

"I don't know what to say. Thank you so much." I clutched it to my chest. "I love that you remembered how much I love this painting."

"We bought that at the Louvre," Kate said. "And the matching T-shirts for you and Ty are from Rome."

Tyler pulled out a shirt from his bag and held it up for me. The photo on the front showed a boy and girl on a Vespa. He walked around the sofa, hugged Kate, then faced Lee. "Thank you, Uncle ... I mean, Lee." Tyler scrunched his features and shook his head.

"That's okay, Ty." Lee ruffled his hair. "You can call me Uncle Lee."

It would be true before long, anyway. Lee had asked my parents for Kate's hand in marriage this past December when we'd flown to Los Angeles to celebrate Christmas with them. My parents had been thrilled. Kate had no idea, and I couldn't wait.

Lee planned to propose on the beach. It was only fitting, for Hawaii. He was getting some last-minute details ready and was waiting on the ring he'd had designed. I hadn't seen it, but knowing his taste, it was going to be beautiful.

I walked to the kitchen counter and grabbed my phone. "Before I forget, let me take a quick picture and send it to Mom." I pointed at my son. "Bridget, stand beside Ty. Say cheese."

"Cheese," everyone said with an exaggerated voice.

I snapped the photo and sent it. Tyler and Bridget went back to eating their desserts and playing their game.

Lee drank his tea and placed it on the coffee table with a light thunk. "Abby, are you free next Saturday? I would like to invite you and Tyler to have dinner at my place. I'm going to barbecue, and the kids can swim in the pool."

Tyler looked up from the tablet. "I want to go." He shrugged sheepishly when I furrowed my brow at him. "I mean, can we please go? It'll be fun." He flashed all his teeth in an exaggerated smile, trying to convince me.

I had turned down Lee's past two dinner invitations, but not because I didn't want to spend time with them. It always felt like pity—like they were asking me so I wouldn't be alone. But I couldn't keep doing it.

"Sure, Ty and I will be there. Thank you for the invite."

Lee gave a curt nod and grinned. "Also, I hope you don't mind that I asked Ian to join us."

My polite smile faltered. This felt like a set-up. And why did my heart beat faster at the thought of seeing Ian again? *Blimey.*

Chapter Three — Four Years

I stood on the threshold of my son's bedroom. "Ty, you ready?"

On the left wall stretched the mural I had painted for him as a birthday request—the night sky with stars on the ceiling and a rocket ship blasting off. Opposite the mural, I had painted bold, bright letters over the dresser that glowed in the dark: *I love you across the galaxies and beyond.* That had become our motto to each other. A reminder that even though I was his only parent, I loved him enough for two people.

Tyler shut the closet door and smiled at me. He tucked the hem of his brown and white checkered T-shirt inside his beige shorts. He looked at the long mirror attached to his closet door and patted his sleeked-back hair.

"Now I'm ready." He grabbed the present I had wrapped last night for Jace.

We walked out to the garage together, hopped in the minivan, and drove off. Jace's parents would supervise Tyler, but this was the first time parents had not been invited to attend. The thought left me so anxious that my chest hurt.

My son was my life. I had to learn to let go. I had to give him space so he could learn to be independent. And I wanted to, but it was a struggle, every day, not to hold him too close.

We pulled up to the house, and my discomfort doubled. Where we lived in a cozy one-story home, Jace's neighborhood had spacious lots and three-story mansions. Manicured front lawns displayed lush green grass and exotic flowers, and even the palm trees looked trimmed and perfect.

I parked on the curb. "Okay, Ty, I'll come pick you up at five. Call me if you want to come home earlier."

"I don't have a phone. How do I call you?" Tyler crossed his arms and hiked an eyebrow.

I dropped my hands from the wheel and pushed the button to unlock the door. "Nice try. You're not getting one until you're at least in junior high. You can ask Jace's mom to call me. Do you want me to walk you, or do you want to go in by yourself?"

Tyler pushed the door open and hopped out with the birthday gift in hand. "I can go myself."

"I love you across the galaxies and beyond," I said, and blew him a kiss. A year ago, I would have gotten out of the car to kiss him, but he wouldn't let me anymore.

"I love you across the galaxies and beyond," he mumbled.

He didn't sound like he meant it, but I took the win and let it go. Soon, maybe even this year, he might not say it back. While he ran across the cobblestone walkway to the grand double front doors, I lowered the passenger side window to see him more clearly.

When the door opened, a mop of auburn peeked out, then Jessica Conner walked out toward her car and waved at me. She must have dropped off Jarrad. I'd first met Jessica and her son at Tyler's preschool. Jarrad had been in Tyler's class last year, but not this year.

Jessica had been all over Lee a few years ago, vying for his attention, but she'd stopped when Lee and Kate got together. She had gotten a divorce right around that time and had seemed intent on getting her paws on rich, eligible bachelors.

I raised a hand to Jessica as I watched Tyler go inside the house, then I drove to the local beach. I should be working, but today was the fourth anniversary of Steve's passing. There was no way I could concentrate.

The soft wind tousled my hair back away from my face as I stepped out of the car. The sun bathing my skin warmed me to the bone. I tucked my small purse under the seat and shoved my keys in the back pocket of my jean shorts.

I slipped off my sandals and let them dangle from my hand. My toes dug into the soft white sand with every step I took toward the ocean. Mist brushed my face as the sea breeze enveloped me, and I licked the hint of salt off my lips.

Families lounged under colorful sun umbrellas while others swam or surfed in the water. Children and parents built sandcastles together. Laughter and chatting rang in the air.

"Look, Mommy, I found it," a boy about four years old said. He held up a small white seashell, water lapping over his feet.

His dark hair and brown eyes reminded me of my son at that age. My heart tugged, then squeezed. The boy's father picked him up as his mother and his younger sister ran up to examine the boy's beach treasure.

That could have been us. If Steve had lived, I would've had another child. A daughter or son to follow Tyler around, adoring him and driving him crazy. I inhaled deeply and veered away from the crowd.

I plunked on the sand, far enough from the water that my butt remained dry and close enough for the water to lap at my toes when I stretched my legs. At first, the cold ocean water stung, but I grew numb to the chilly splashes. Wearing only shorts and a tank top, I should have lathered on sunscreen, but I didn't have any, and I couldn't bring myself to care that much.

Tyler used to love looking for seashells with me, but lately, he'd lost interest. He had stopped crawling onto my bed in the early morning—had stopped doing a lot of things, actually. It only meant he was growing up.

Whipped-cream clouds floated overhead, and the endless water sparkled like crystals. It reminded me of a painting I had finished recently. As I dug my toes into the wet sand, memories of Steve crashed over me like waves—how we'd met, our wedding, Tyler's birth, and when he'd told me about his cancer. We had cried in each other's arms that night.

We had been so young once, thinking we had a whole life ahead of us. But fate had different plans. After he died, I'd wanted to remember every moment we'd had together. That regret made it even harder to let Ty have the independence he craved.

I spoke to Steve in my mind.

It's been four years since you left us. It seems long ago, and yet it seems like it happened yesterday. Sometimes I don't know if I can go on … I paused to dab the tears edging at the corners of my eyes. *But Tyler gives me the will and strength. I live for him, and though I hear you saying I need to live for myself, too, it's hard, especially when I see other families doing things we should be doing.*

I have no right to be mad, and I know I'm not the only single mother or the only widow in the world, but it sucks. This sucks so much. I miss you, Steve. I miss you so much.

Tears streamed down my face, and I wiped them away. I wrapped my arms around my bended knees and rocked until I had no tears left.

I scooped up wet sand and dumped it next to me with a damp plop to distract myself. I did it again, creating a pile as I spoke to my dead husband.

To be honest, I've been a horrible daughter-in-law. I should call your mother and your sister more often, but it hurts, so I don't. They remind me of you. And then it takes a while to pick myself back up.

The tide crept closer and flicked water on me. I rose quickly and dusted sand off the back of my shorts. As I clapped my hands to shake off the rest, something flashed white in the tumbling water.

I ran to it and picked it up before it could get lost in the wave, intending to add a seashell from this day to my tabletop collection. I dusted sand off the ridged surface and examined it—two perfect clamshells attached side by side at the top, with an elegant shape, long and narrowing at the bottom with grooves radiating from the top corner.

It looked like an angel's wings, about the size of my fist with lines across it from one end to the other. I had never seen such an extraordinary seashell before.

I curled my fingers around the edges, and my spirit immediately lifted. It felt like a gift from Steve, telling me to be strong and that everything would be fine. And a sign of good things to come. I brought it close to my heart and closed my eyes, then icy water shot up my thighs. With a yelp, I kicked the water again and again, laughing.

People stared at me, so I backed away, picked up my sandals, and walked back to my parked minivan. I stopped by Izzy's Café, a coffee shop located inside a small shopping center on the way home. A bell chimed when I entered.

Izzy's green eyes rounded, and she wiggled her sharp nose when she saw me. She smiled brighter than the sun pouring through the windows.

"Hello, Izzy." I inhaled the smell of fresh ground coffee and stopped at one of the round wooden tables.

In the far back corner by a surfboard on the wall, a couple shared a slab of chocolate cake and sipped from paper cups. I frowned and approached the counter so I wouldn't have to see them. Usually, seeing couples didn't bother me, but today wasn't like other days. A coffee shop at the university had been where I'd met Steve Fuller.

"Good afternoon, Abby," Izzy said in her usual chirpy tone. "I'm happy to see you."

Her skin crinkled at the corners of her eyes, and the crease on her forehead deepened when she offered a warm smile and a wave at a departing customer. Years in Hawaii had left her fair skin with a golden glow and a lifetime of smile lines. They looked good on her.

I placed my hands on the wood counter near a net tangled with starfishes and seashells. The clam reminded me of the one I had found today and left on my passenger seat.

"Tyler went to a birthday party, and I had some time, so I thought I'd treat myself to a hazelnut latte."

"With soy milk and one pump." Not a question, but to confirm, instead.

I had ordered the same latte, made the same way, for the past four years.

"Anything else?" She dusted white powder off her loose olive-green shirt and poked at the tablet to put in my order.

I peered over her head at the blackboard menu. Nothing appealed to me, so I stepped over to the glass display cabinet—chocolate cake, mango muffins, and macadamia nut cookies.

"Give me half a dozen of the cookies. Tyler and I can have them for dessert."

"How's my favorite good-looking boy?"

"He's good. He's at his first birthday party without me."

Izzy snorted. "Get used to it."

I didn't need her to explain what she meant.

While Izzy made my latte, I glanced about the small, airy space. The paneled walls hung with island gear—surfboard, scuba fins, old-fashioned snorkeling gear. The couple had left, and there was no one else but Izzy and me. The latte machine growled and whirred in the background, and I thought about more Saturdays without Tyler at my side.

"Here you go." Izzy placed a paper cup and a brown wax-paper bag with the cookies on the counter.

I took a sip and savored the soothing warmth that spread down my throat, the sweet flavor awakening my taste buds. "You make the best lattes."

She smiled, but it didn't reach her eyes.

"What's wrong?" I asked.

She rested her elbow on the counter and propped her chin on her fist. "Nothing wrong with me, but something isn't right with you. There's no one here, so tell me."

Aside from my sister, there weren't many people who asked about me, about how I was feeling. My days were spent taking care of others. But Izzy was like an older sister. She knew about Steve, so I told her why today was harder than other days and where I had been.

"I'm so sorry, Abby." Her eyes were gentle and kind.

I tapped a finger on my paper cup and let out a slow sigh. "We were married the same number of years he's been gone. That seems important, somehow. I'm okay most days, but the anniversary of his death, the birthdays, and the holidays are the hardest."

The Seashell of ʻOhana

Izzy caressed my shoulder over the counter with an empathetic smile. "I can't promise the pain will go away, but it will get easier with time. Love never dies, Abby. He's always with you, watching out for you and Ty. One day, you'll love someone else, and even then, Steve will always be with you."

I couldn't see myself with any other man, but I gave her a tight-lipped grin. When another customer entered, I slipped out.

Chapter Four — Carousel Gallery

One of the perks of owning your own gallery is being the boss, which means making your own schedule. After dropping Tyler off at school, I headed to Carousel Art Gallery. Seeing my sign over my own gallery, even after four years, still gave me a thrill of pride.

Wind chimes tinkled the air when I pushed through the double glass door into the open, well-lit space. The sound tugged my heartstrings and soothed my soul. My muscles eased, my spirits lifted.

When Kate had become part-owner of the gallery about three years ago, she'd insisted we install a doorbell that sounded like wind chimes. I hadn't asked her about it, but I suspected it brought up similar memories for us both.

Our mother always hung wind chimes in the backyard. Kate used to sit back there to read, especially on sunny days with a gentle breeze. She had told me once that wind chimes sounded like angel wings to her. I always thought of that when I heard them.

"Good morning, Stella." I passed the reception desk and the two white leather sofas in the center of the room and headed to the table under a large-scale photograph of a sea turtle on the sandy beach.

Stella pulled her mug away from her mouth. "Good morning, Abby. I started the process from yesterday's online purchases. I'll get those sent out through UPS. And we got more orders this morning."

"Good. Thanks." I picked up the insulated paper cup, poured hot water from the coffeemaker, and dunked a passion fruit green tea bag inside.

Stella's fingers moved along the keyboard in a flurry of clicks. "You've got a full schedule today." She clicked some more. "Well, this week. Actually, the whole month."

"Good, I need all those clients so I can keep paying you." I chuckled and blew on the fragrant steam rising from my cup.

I relaxed in the ambient glow from the sunlight pouring through the front window over the sculptures of angels, seashells, and turtles on shelves. I took a long, slow sip. God, that felt good. The hot liquid soothed my throat, and the bitter taste jolted my senses. The first taste was always heaven.

Stella flashed all her teeth with an exaggerated grin. "You can always give me a raise."

I hiked an eyebrow. "You just got one recently."

She shrugged. "I can always use another."

I cleared my throat and narrowed my eyes at her. "Kate should be here soon," I murmured, and moved to stand in front of the new paintings Kate and I had hung before she'd left for vacation.

We had replaced the ones we'd sold with close replicas of two popular landscapes: *Tree Tunnel,* a dreamy portrayal of the eucalyptus tree tunnel on Maluhia Road, and *Wailua Falls,* a rainbow arched over a lush mountain and sparkling waterfall. Farther along the stark white wall hung an assortment of landscapes, portraits, and abstracts in oil and acrylic. Wood carvings displayed on white pedestals under soft lighting dotted the room.

Stella stopped typing and swiveled her rolling desk chair toward me. The sunlight caught the red highlights in her dark hair and lit her gray eyes with an extra sparkle. In her pink lacy shirt and long jean skirt, she looked younger than her early twenties.

"Kate is already here," she said. "She's in the back."

"Oh. Let me know if you need anything." My voice came out chirpy, and my mood changed from heavy to light. I readjusted my purse strap over my shoulder and strolled to the back, the paper mug warm in my grasp.

I'd thought Stella would quit after a few months, but when our gallery had gotten busy, I'd given her a raise. Weeks had turned to months, and months turned to years. Though she mentioned grad school from time to time, she hadn't left me yet.

Over the years, Stella had become like a younger sister to Kate and me. With only the three of us working so closely together, we confided in each other and had developed a more personal relationship.

I dropped my purse on the desk in the back room and set down the paper mug. I stepped up to the easel holding my latest painting, which I'd set aside for a charity auction, before shifting my attention to my sister.

Kate sat on a stool in front of another easel near the red storage shelf at the back of the room, painting a landscape of Kauai. Despite new ventilation, the pungent fumes of oil paints and thinners filled the room. She wore jeans and a T-shirt underneath her painting apron, with her long hair tied in a low ponytail. She kept painting, oblivious to me lurking behind her.

The sight took me back to our college years. We would paint through the night, taking short naps in between to finish our projects. Those had been wonderful years. And who would have thought we would both go from USC in Los Angeles to living in Kauai?

Kate had earbuds in, and her whole body moved as if the music flowed to the canvas through her arm. Her paintbrush stroked across in feathery moves, creating a lifelike ocean in the twilight.

She had captured the sunset gleaming across the water. The couple walking hand-in-hand on the white sand reminded me of Lee and Kate. And the hues of pink and violet across the sky perfectly matched Kauai's breathtaking evening skies.

I inched closer, drawn in by the combination of rich colors that brought the scene to life. And just as I was about to tap her shoulder, Kate stretched her arms back to yawn, and something cold squished on my face.

"Not again." Kate jumped out of her chair. "What are you doing sneaking up on me like that? Make some noise next time, will you? You'll give me a heart attack, and then you won't have a painting partner."

Not again? Kate had never gotten paint on me before, but she had smeared Lee on several occasions.

I would have laughed had she not made a big deal about it, but her prissy mood annoyed me. Kate had been living with me until about a year ago, when she'd bought a cute little bungalow, and it had been good for both of us. We got along, but she needed her own space.

I rolled my eyes and went to the restroom mirror to assess my face. "You should either turn the volume down or not use earbuds." I scrubbed the oil paint soap into my right cheek and splashed it with cool water, then watched the sudsy violet liquid swirl down the sink.

I caught my sister's reflection in the mirror when I peered up.

Kate crossed her arms and leaned on her hip. "Sorry. I didn't mean to … you scared me. And—"

I raised a hand to cut her off and dabbed my cheek with a paper towel. "It's fine. We're both tired and busy. I think we should hire another person or two. We're so swamped. And Stella just told me we got more online orders."

"Yeah, and that's great," Kate said. "But at the rate we're going, it'll be months before those commissions are fulfilled."

I walked out to the tall metal storage shelf crowded with bins full of tube paints and brushes, next to ones holding break-room supplies.

"I'll tell Stella to get this process started and line up the interviews," I said.

I grabbed a canvas from the pile on the small table, propped it on my wooden easel next to Kate's, then gathered the oil paints and lined them up for easy access next to my palette. From the bin on the shelf, I took out brushes and layered color on the image in front of me.

Kate cleared her throat. "So, are you going to tell me about that kiss?"

I knew she would ask sooner or later, but there wasn't much to say. So why was my face burning?

"What kiss?" I mixed a dab of white into the blue sky on the canvas.

"Oh, you know. When Ian kissed you at the market." Kate swiped pink across the clouds on her canvas. "Were you going to tell me about it? Or were you never going to share?"

I put the paintbrush on the tray next to me. "You're making it out to be a big deal, and it isn't. He happened to be at the market and caught me just before I fell. We exchanged a few words, and then he gave me a quick peck on the cheek before he left. That's all. The end. He didn't ask me out, and we didn't exchange phone numbers. Not that I would go out with him."

I felt like I was in college, talking about boys and dating stuff all over again.

"Why not?" Kate whirled on the stool to face me and narrowed her eyes. "Ian is a great guy. Why wouldn't you date him?"

"*You* date him." After I said it, I realized how childish that sounded. The door swung open, cutting off our heated conversation.

Stella walked in. "Can I order lunch now?"

Kate and I often forgot to eat, so Stella helped keep us fed by ordering lunch sometimes.

"Yes!" Kate and I barked an answer at the same time.

"Whoa." Stella put out her hands. "I'm just the messenger. Tension much?"

"Sorry." Kate and I spoke again at the same time, but softer.

"Whatever. I'm glad I don't work with my sister," she said, and walked out, the door slamming behind her.

"I'm already in love with someone else," Kate stressed.

Three years ago, when Kate had come to visit me during Christmas, she'd taken a job as a nanny for two weeks. I'd thought my sister had gone crazy. Why on earth would she get a job as a nanny, two weeks or not, when she had a career as a graphic designer?

I'd found out that she'd done it to help me financially—the job's fee of four grand for two weeks would've tempted almost anyone. Still, I'd hated having my little sister feel like she needed to take care of me.

As it had turned out, her taking that job was kismet. It was how she'd met Lee and Bridget, how they'd fallen in love. Lee had wanted my sister to stay here in Kauai, so he'd asked me to organize a showing of Kate's paintings so he could present them to his friends and his real estate business partners. Afterward, our business skyrocketed. That exhibition had changed Kate's life and saved my gallery.

Kate wiped her brush and then swirled it inside a small bottle of turpentine on her rolling tray. The pink pigment dissolved into the smelly liquid, leaving the brush clean. She turned back to her canvas and dabbed black on the blue ocean to add depth.

"I'm sorry." She waved her brush when I kept my lips sealed. "Kauai is a small dating pool, and Ian is a good man. I've gotten to know him because of Lee. Lee told me Ian has a good heart, and I see it through his actions. Besides, he's great with kids. I don't mean to push him on you. Only *you* know when you can move on."

Unexpected tears pooled in my eyes. The combination of missing Steve, Tyler's increasing push for independence, and the attraction to Ian that I couldn't comprehend cracked the wall I usually kept around myself. Especially at work.

I blinked to keep the tears at bay, but let out a funny squawk of dismay, and the dam broke.

"Abby. Abby." Soft arms wrapped around me. "I'm so sorry. I said too much."

Apologies made it worse. My sister was only looking out for me, and I'd gotten all defensive. My face was a snotty mess of tears, and emotions flew in all directions. It was unlike me to lose control.

It will pass. Just like everything else. Everything will be fine.

"It's okay." I choked back a sob and wiped my tears. "I'm sorry I snapped at you. I haven't been myself lately. It's probably hormonal."

Kate offered a heartfelt smile. The smile said, in a thousand words, that she was there for me no matter what … the way she had *always* been.

"This is nothing. We've had worse fights." She handed me a paper towel. "Want me to come over to your place tonight? We can share a bucket of ice cream."

A memory surfaced of the time in high school when my boyfriend had broken up with me. We had only dated for a few months, but he had been my first heartache. And like every heartsick teenager, I'd thought it was the end of my life.

Kate and I had gone through a gallon of coffee ice cream, and afterward, I'd felt so much better. Of course, it hadn't been the ice cream, but my sister who had made me laugh through the tears and realize there was so much life ahead of me. There would be more bumps in the road, and I had to learn to manage them.

Life is a journey. Some roads will curve, but it's up to me to walk straight.

"I'm fine," I said. "Don't worry."

Kate probably had plans with Lee. He would be fine if she told him I needed company, but I didn't want to intrude. Besides, the tears had done their job and washed away my frustrations.

Her lips twisted, and she made a small noise of disbelief. Kate went to the small fridge by the shelf and pulled out a tub of coffee ice cream. She took three paper bowls and three plastic spoons from the bin.

"When did you—"

"Yesterday. I felt like some," she said.

Kate and I usually had a junk food stash on hand for when we were having a creative crisis. Chips, chocolate, and cookies, but not ice cream.

"Why three?" I asked.

She tugged me off my stool. "Because we need to apologize to Stella. We don't want her looking for another job."

"Did she say something?" I matched her pace and opened the door.

"No, but she knows how busy we are, and she knows way too much about our business. The gallery isn't rocket science, but she'd be hard to replace."

Sometimes we were too comfortable with Stella and forgot to treat her like an employee. Like, how we'd snapped at her. I had to remember she wasn't a blood sister, no matter how much I adored her. I would be saddened if she left us for another job. It would be like losing a family member.

"Stella. It's break time." Kate's voice filled the room, and she set the ice cream tub on Stella's desk.

"Come to apologize, have you?" Stella crossed her arms, waggling her eyebrows playfully.

Ice cream did make everything better. When had Kate become the older sister? It seemed like our roles had reversed.

Chapter Five — Saturday at Lee's

"Mom, let's go." Tyler stood by the garage door, fidgeting. He'd been ready to go to Lee's house since that morning.

I moved the phone away from my mouth. "Just a minute, Ty. I'm on the phone with your grandmother. I'll be right there." I put my mom on the speaker and shuffled to my room. "I gotta go, Mom. I'll call you later. Say hi to Dad for me."

I tossed the phone on my bed and went to the bathroom.

My parents had put up their house for sale to move to Kauai. It made sense, as Kate and I had settled here with no plans for moving back to Los Angeles. I had been speaking with a realtor, and Kate and I planned to help our parents find the perfect affordable house near us.

I fluffed my dark hair in front of the mirror and watched it fall in a gentle wave to my shoulder blades. After gliding on plum lip gloss, I tucked my white short-sleeve shirt inside my jeans. As I kneeled on the hardwood floor to rummage through the swim bag by the closet, I went through a mental list of things I should have already packed.

One extra swimsuit for Tyler. He already had one on.

Sunscreen. Check. Already put some on Tyler.

An extra pair of goggles.

Two swim towels. Yup.

My wallet. No need to bring a purse.

Change of clothes for Tyler after swimming.

Change of clothes for me, just in case.

My knuckles hit something hard, so I shoved the two bulky towels to the side. Tyler's tablet? I hadn't put that there.

"Ty, you don't need to take your tablet," I hollered. "I'm not packing it."

Quick footsteps pattered down the hall toward my room. Tyler scrunched his face in defiance and tugged on the hem of his green T-shirt, which matched the palm tree print on his swim trunks.

"Argh, Mom," he said with a huff, swinging a pair of goggles like a spinning toy. "I want to take it so Bridget and I can play."

When my parents had bought the device for Tyler several Christmases ago, I wasn't happy about it, but I had to admit it came in handy when I needed to keep him busy in restaurants or at home. But I'd never allowed him to take it to social gatherings, and I wasn't about to start.

"Stop swinging that thing. And you don't need the tablet." I got up and dropped it on my bed.

He strapped his goggles over his head and opened his mouth to say something, most likely to argue, but instead, he let out a defeated breath. "Aye—but can we hurry?"

I shouldered the bag, shoved my phone in my back jeans pocket, and walked out of my room. "I just need to grab the cake, and we're all set."

Tyler rushed off to the garage before I could say another word.

As many times as I had been to Lee's mansion, I marveled at the beautiful modern architecture and the grandness of the structure every time I drove up the curvy cobblestone driveway. Plus, the home was nestled on a private beach. It must be nice to wake up to a breathtaking ocean view and swaying palm trees.

I inhaled the salty, fresh ocean breeze, temporarily distracted by a couple strolling on the sand. Dogs on leashes trotted beside their owners, and families built sandcastles. Some people paddled on surfboards and kids ran away from the water, gushing over their feet.

"Can I hold the dessert for you, Mom?" Tyler asked as we walked together to the front door.

Sometimes Tyler acted like a child, as he should, but he never failed to offer to hold things for me and was quick to help others.

Yellow, white, and red hibiscus bloomed on either side of the walkway, their sweet scent spiraling around me.

When Tyler pressed the doorbell, I inhaled a deep breath. Why did I feel so nervous?

One of the double grand doors opened to reveal Mona—the nanny, housekeeper, and do-it-all woman. She greeted us with the warmest smile, her blue eyes gleaming. She wore an oversized flower print dress that brushed against her ankles, and her hair was tied back into a tight bun. Kate had said Mona was in her late fifties, but she looked young for her age, aside from the stark-white hair.

"Come in. Come in." Mona ushered us inside and hugged us under the dancing light from a crystal chandelier. "Let me take those off your hands. They're in the backyard. Go ahead."

She grabbed the dessert from Tyler, but I held up a hand to stop her when she reached for my bag.

"I can carry it." I smiled.

I felt uncomfortable letting people do things for me, and I certainly didn't want someone older carrying things I could easily manage. And I also wanted it to be a teachable moment for Tyler—take care of yourself and help others. Kids learned from actions and not just by words, so I always knew how he'd see me.

"Don't swim in the deep end," I hollered after him when Tyler ran off. He had taken swimming lessons and was a good swimmer, but I still worried.

I padded across the beige marble floor. The high ceiling and grand sweeping staircase always made me feel so small after the coziness of my house. To get to the backyard, I passed the family room, which was three times the size of mine. Over the mantel hung a portrait of Lee, Bridget, and Kate.

I went through the dream kitchen—complete with white cabinets and cream granite counters. Not a spot stained the stove. I wondered if they had a side kitchen, as if this one was just for show.

All the appliances were stainless steel and state of the art, top quality. They reminded me of my apartment in New York where Steve, Tyler, and I had lived for a year. Our first home.

Steve had purchased a top-of-the-line brand while I'd wanted to save money. He had gotten his job as a financial analyst and wanted to provide the best for the family. He had been a proud man.

Nostalgia hit me so hard, I almost forgot where I was.

"Mom, this way." Tyler peeked in from the sliding door.

When Tyler took off without me, I didn't expect to see him again until I went to the backyard, but he had gone to get his aunt. My sister waved through the glass. She looked cute in a cream sundress and matching sandals.

I went out through the glass double doors. Palm trees lined either side of the walkway. Upbeat music blasted from the outside speakers. A three-tiered gray stone fountain gurgled in the center.

The front yard was breathtaking with the view of the ocean, but the backyard was an island oasis on its own. I followed Kate past the firepit and under an awning that shaded a set of sofas.

"Abby, welcome." Lee waved with a stainless-steel spatula. He was cooking at the built-in barbecue, wearing khaki shorts and a gray tank top.

I rushed over with Kate and hugged him. "Thanks for inviting us and for cooking."

"It's my pleasure. I don't do it that often, so enjoy." He chuckled and wiped the sweat beading on his forehead with his arm.

The aroma of steak and chicken on the grill made my stomach rumble. I hadn't eaten much for lunch. Kate and I had agreed we would take today off, but I had gone into the gallery that morning.

"Relax by the pool while I finish up here," Lee said, and flipped the steaks. Fat sizzled, sending a fresh wave of enticing smells my way.

Kate went around the barbecue to a minibar and came back. "Here. Lee made this for us just before you arrived." She handed me a tall, cold glass with a straw and a little colorful umbrella. "It's a piña colada."

"My favorite. Thank you." I raised the drink to Lee, took a long, sweet sip, and walked past a garden filled with a somehow-tidy riot of rose bushes, orange plumeria, yellow hibiscus, and birds of paradise. The swimming pool lay just beyond it, already ringing with children's shouts and splashing.

I placed the duffel bag on a wooden lounge chair covered with a bright cushion. As a soft breeze lifted strands of hair to caress my back, I took another sip of the fruity drink. The wind left me to whisper in the tops of coconut trees and amid the tall pampas grass behind the pool.

"Walk the plank, mate." I heard Bridget's voice.

"Aye, aye, Captain. Mom!" Tyler waved and slid down the super cool slide.

He splashed into the water, and I remained standing, waiting. He swiped water off his face and fixed his goggles when he resurfaced. I exhaled.

Even after years of swimming lessons, the mother instinct tugged at my core and told me to wait until he was safe. Call me paranoid, but recent news of kids drowning in their backyards had me even more on edge.

"Hello, Abby." Bridget waved, her one-piece pink swimsuit sparkling like mermaid scales against the sunlight.

Seeing Bridget without anything related to unicorns, which used to be on almost everything she owned, made me long for those days. When Tyler had lost interest in his building blocks, it had been one of the saddest moments in my motherhood journey. The kids were growing up too fast.

Something caught my eye. No, not something. Someone. A tall, handsome, and tanned man, with six-pack abs and a whole lot of muscles, splashed out of the water and walked up the stairs. Water dripped from his hair and streamed down his chest. One rivulet snaked lower, and I yanked my gaze upward. He raked his hair back with both hands, flexing his toned biceps as his lips curled wickedly into a sexy smirk.

Shiver me timbers.

A drop of cold water slipped off my glass and over my knuckle. I needed more than that to cool me down, and I needed to stop staring. Maybe I needed CPR. He looked like a daydream, but he was real. And he ... was Ian Bordonaro.

Ian made water footprints toward a pool chair, grabbed the towel slung over it, and dragged it over his hair, chest, and black swim trunks. Then he draped the towel around his neck and strutted toward me.

My heart pounded and my feet grew roots into the poolside concrete. His presence captured me, and those lips curled upward to let me know he was happy to see me—that grin nearly undid me.

"Abby. You're here." Ian wrapped his arms around my shoulders and planted a smooch just beside my lips.

That kiss ignited in my belly and warmed me down to my toes.

Despite his cool face brushing against my cheek and his wet body touching mine, my temperature spiked to blazing hot. And I might have forgotten how to breathe. My gaze tunneled into his gorgeous, brooding eyes. I wondered what secrets he held in them when he pulled away.

An artist never missed the smallest details, something that had been ingrained in me. Sometimes, I'd forget where I was and would study someone a bit longer than necessary. Like now.

"Hello, Ian." I managed to get my tongue moving and offered an affable smile.

"It's good to see you. Lee told me you were coming." His gaze traveled to the glass in my hand.

"How have you been?" I didn't know what else to say. It had been so long since I'd socialized with a man for any purpose other than a business transaction.

Not a dumb question. You're doing just fine.

"I've been relaxing and taking some time off from work. And I see you're drinking one of Lee's famous cocktails. Sometimes he's a little too generous with the rum, but don't tell him I said that. Might hurt his pride." He winked.

If I hadn't been acting like a schoolgirl with a crush before, I was surely flushing after that wink. But Ian might be right. I could already feel the effects of the alcohol. My neck blazed. Or maybe it was from his gaze, roaming every inch of me.

I took another drink and craned my neck to the pool. My gaze landed on the perfect distraction of Bridget and Tyler with their arms over the floating noodles, staring up at Ian and me, smiling. Ian ruffled his hair with the towel, and it took every ounce of my will not to stare at him. He must lift weights and exercise every single day of the year to be that fit.

"Time to eat," Kate called.

Thank God.

"I'll see you at the table. I'm going to give Ty his towel," I said when it seemed like he was waiting for me to take the first step.

"Then I'll take your drink to the table for you," he said.

I passed my glass to him and pulled the beach towel out of the duffel bag. After Tyler came out of the water, I wrapped a towel around him.

"*Mom*, I can do it." He wiggled out of my hold and held out his hand for the towel.

I needed to keep in mind that he wasn't five years old anymore, and he liked to do things for himself. But doting on him made me happy, and going the extra mile had given me something to focus on when grief had become too much. I trailed behind the kids to the dining table under an awning and eased onto the only empty chair beside Ian.

My piña colada sat next to a thick white paper plate and utensils. Napkins and water bottles were set in the center. Ian had put on a tank top, but kept his swim trunks on.

Kate had already prepared the kids' plates, and they ate at a separate table, closer to the pool.

"Ty, eat your vegetables." I pointed at his plate. "Take a bite of the broccoli. Just try it."

"Mom." He waved a hand.

I sighed and picked up a plate and utensils from the table. I forked up some steak, a corn on the cob, and a few helpings of asparagus and broccoli. Everyone else did the same.

"Everything looks great," I said to Lee.

"If it doesn't taste good, then blame it on Ian." Lee chuckled as he sliced a knife across the ribeye steak, revealing a stripe of pink under the perfectly browned exterior.

"Lee blames all his failures on me." Ian grinned and bit into the asparagus he held between his fingers.

I glanced between Lee and Ian. "Kate told me you two grew up together?"

Ian gulped his beer. "We did, and our parents are close. They vacationed once a year together."

"That's so sweet." I cut a thin slice and sank my teeth into the tender, juicy meat.

"Lee is like a brother to me. We've been best friends since we were in diapers."

"Yup, he's my diaper friend." Lee flashed a warm grin and held up a beer bottle at Ian. "We've been there for each other through so many things. From first broken hearts to nursing each other when one of us drank too much and had to spend the night hugging the porcelain goddess."

We shared a laugh.

"Porcelain goddess?" I crinkled my nose and took a sip of my piña colada.

"The toilet." Ian shrugged sheepishly. "Lee and I partied a lot in college."

Kate and I never drank heavily, nor had we gone to parties. We'd taken our studies seriously. And I'd started dating Steve during my junior year in college, so Steve was all I knew.

Kate snickered and picked up an asparagus spear from her plate. "They're just like us, Abby. They went to the same preschool, elementary, junior high, high school, even attended the same college and majored in business together."

"Well, I think that's special." I picked up the corn and immediately dropped it. My fingertips blazed like I had put my hand over the fire. I wasn't expecting it to be that hot.

Lee handed me a corn skewer from the basket by the end of the table. "Here, use these. Sorry, I should have told you it was still hot."

"Thanks." I pushed the spiky part in, but I couldn't get a good grip.

Ian leaned closer. "Let me help you."

I stiffened when our elbows and then our knees touched under the table. I moved over to give him room.

"These darn things can be slippery." He forked the skewer on both sides while letting out a grunt. "There."

We held each other's gaze as I thanked him. I looked away first and took a bite. Sweet and crunchy, just the way I like it. When I turned my attention to Kate, she smiled with her head lowered like she was trying to hide it.

Because I knew her so well, I didn't have to guess that she was thinking about Ian and me. That brat. I laughed inwardly and ignored her. I kicked her pretty sandals under the table when she wouldn't stop snickering.

"Ouch. What was that for?" Kate sounded as if I'd really hurt her.

Lee and Ian glanced between Kate and me.

I shrugged. "Sorry. It was an accident." I bore my gaze into hers, then looked past Kate to the kids' table to check on Tyler.

He was eating and talking to Bridget while they watched something on her tablet. As we continued our meal, we talked about politics, parents, and about the kids and how fast they were growing up.

The sun dipped lower, replaced by the moon and the stars. Outdoor lights brightened the areas under the awning, the pool, and around the garden. The lights cast shadows and highlights that made the scene beautiful in an entirely new way. I felt like I had been transported to a posh resort.

Mona came out with a tray of desserts I had brought—chocolate cake with strawberries in the middle—already cut and placed on the plates with a plastic fork. We thanked her as she handed a plate to each of us.

"Bridget asked if she could have a cell phone the other day." As Lee furrowed his eyebrows, he stabbed a fork through the strawberry and took a bite. "Can you believe that?" He glanced at the kids, who were eating dessert and laughing at something on the tablet.

"What did you tell her?" Ian looked at me. "This is so good."

Lee took a sip of his beer. "I told her if she can pay her monthly phone bill, then she can get one."

Ian chuckled. "Technically, she can. If she finds out she has a trust fund, you'll never hear the end of it."

"I plan to hold onto that until she goes to college, or maybe after she's twenty-one. Or at least when she's mature enough to handle that much money."

I swallowed the rich, chocolatey bite and licked my lips, trying to get at a dab of cool frosting I felt at the corner of my mouth. "Ty asked me the same. A few kids in their class have one. Can you believe it?"

"I do." Ian narrowed his eyes.

He reached over to my face, and at the same time, I reached toward him to wipe white cream off his chin, but then put my hand down.

"You have frosting on your ..." He gently smeared a thumb across my lips, meeting my gaze with something warm and inviting.

I turned away and forked a big chunk of the cake.

"Anyway ..." Kate cleared her throat. "How about we play ping-pong after dessert?"

Kate, what are you thinking? But I stayed quiet because ping-pong was better than going swimming. And my dear sister, who knew me well, would assume I hadn't brought a swimsuit.

"Ping-pong?" Ian's lips tugged at the corner, and his eyes gleamed when he looked at Lee.

"I can't wait." Lee waggled his brows in challenge.

Kate and I exchanged glances and laughed. They were competitive like us.

Chapter Six — Ping~Pong

After dinner, Kate and Lee went inside to wash the dishes while Ian and I tidied up. I walked around the outdoor dining table, pushing the chairs in until Mona gently placed a hand on my shoulder.

"This is my job, Ms. Abby. You go have fun. Lee tried to teach me ping-pong, but I gave up. I can't follow the ball fast enough." The corner of her eyes crinkled, and the crease on her forehead deepened when she snickered.

"Are you sure?" Being a mother and the firstborn, picking up after others came naturally. I wasn't used to having someone clean up after me.

"Yes, I'm sure. And that goes for you, too, Mr. Ian. Don't you dare pick up that plate." Her tone was stern, all business.

Ian's lips twisted upward as he threw a used napkin into the trash can by the bar. "Yes, ma'am. You're the boss."

"Hurry up, you two," Lee called from the ping-pong table.

Ian and I exchanged a smile and walked over together. There was nothing to clean up, so I didn't mind leaving Mona. She headed back inside anyway.

White lights coiled around the palm trees, and outdoor lighting illuminated the surrounding area. Even the swimming pool lit up with color-changing lights. The soft waterfall added the illusion of a rainbow inside the water.

While Tyler and Bridget sat on the lounge chair to watch, Kate and Lee were on one side of the table. I guessed that meant Ian and I were a team. No matter. It was just a game.

Ian handed me a paddle. "Lee has the ball. He'll serve first. What are we playing for?"

One thing about men, I'd come to realize, was that even playing a simple game was about competition. They had to play for something. I didn't mind it. Kate and I would do the same when we were younger, usually over something like washing the dishes or doing the laundry.

"The losing team has to make dinner for the next gathering." Kate looked at Lee to confirm.

I angled an eyebrow at her. Losing team? Ian and I were a team. If we lost, we would have to cook together. What was my sister thinking?

"Do you agree, Abby?" Ian twirled his paddle with a flick of his wrist like a pro.

What a sweet man, to ask. "Sure. But don't worry. We won't lose."

Ian's lips tugged into a sly grin. "I like this side of you."

I flushed. Ian's words threw me off a bit, but I got my head in the game when Lee served. The white plastic ball bounced once on his square, went over the net in a blur, and pelted at me.

My paddle smacked into the plastic ball with a loud, echoing crack and slammed across to Kate. She volleyed back to me. Ian threw a backhand. Then Lee crushed a fast one on my side. I leaped and slatted right on the white line toward Kate. She couldn't react fast enough. Her paddle swiped at empty air, and she spun around.

"Score!" Ian exclaimed with excitement, and raised a hand for a high five.

"Yah!" Tyler jumped out of his seat and gave me a fist bump, then Ian.

Lee served again and scowled when the ball hit the net.

"That's okay, Lee. Do it again," Kate encouraged.

"Yeah. Don't give up," Bridget said.

Lee hit the ball just barely over the net on my side. I dove for it, my chest landing on the table, but I missed. I had been seconds too slow.

"Sh—cra—oooops." I almost said *shit*, then *crap*, and tried to fix it, but when I glanced at the kids, who were looking back at me with wide eyes—well, too late. They understood what I'd almost said.

"Good effort, Abby." Ian patted his paddle with mine rapidly as if we were clapping. "That's okay. It's only one-to-one." Ian narrowed his eyes at Lee. "Do your worst."

Lee served, fast and hard. Ian hit back. Kate returned. I slammed the ball in front of Lee, and he swung a second late.

"Woo hoo." Ian swung me around unexpectedly. "Take that, Lee."

Lee didn't hesitate to serve, and Ian and I almost missed the return. He dropped the theatrics, and we all settled in for a serious game. Before I knew it, we had won—eleven to nine.

"Better start thinking about that pot roast you're going to make, Lee," Ian teased, and took a sip of his beer from the bottle on the side table.

Lee flipped the paddle like a pro in his hand, his eyes focused on the table. "You haven't won yet. That's only the first round. Stop talking and serve the damn ball."

"Here." Ian held the ball in front of me. "Air kiss for good luck."

I hesitated, then puckered up and blew a kiss.

Ian served to Kate's side. The ball moved so fast. I couldn't follow it. She missed and gaped at Lee. "Sorry."

"That's okay, babe." He placed a gentle kiss on her forehead.

The sweetest sight. Even sweeter, Ian leaned closer so only I could hear. "You're my good luck charm."

I gave him a warm smile and flushed again when Kate hiked an eyebrow at me. I'd have some explaining to do later.

Lee drained the last of his beer and Kate sipped her drink, but I'd stopped, since I had to drive home. Lee had told me that Tyler and I could spend the night—they had plenty of extra bedrooms—but I didn't want to impose. Besides, I was a creature of habit. I preferred sleeping in my bed.

"Can Bridget and I go swimming now?" Tyler tugged on my shirt. "Mom? Mom."

Bridget was patiently waiting for Tyler, both of their gazes on me. I had stressed that the kids had to wait at least half an hour after they finished their dinner.

Under different circumstances, I wouldn't let Tyler swim after dinner, especially on a cool spring evening, but the pool was heated. I had no excuse.

"Okay. Just be careful." I gave him a quick kiss, then turned to the game.

Lee and Kate won the second round. We were on the last game, and Ian and I were a point behind. Occasionally, Kate and I would glance at the kids in the pool. They had been swimming at the shallow end as I had asked, so I didn't worry much.

"We've got this," I said.

My competitive side rose with confidence. I had gotten used to having Ian as my teammate, so the interaction of high fives and slapping our paddles came naturally and easily.

"All right. This is it, for the game." Lee twisted his lips in concentration. "If we score, we win. If you score, then it's a tie. And then we keep—"

"Stop talking," Ian chuckled. "You're stalling."

"Slam it, Lee." Kate scowled and brandished her paddle.

My sister had the cutest challenging glare.

As I swung from left to right, getting my momentum ready, I

flashed a glance over to the pool as I had done every few minutes. But this time ... my heart shot up to my throat, blood rushing in my ears, and I dropped my paddle.

"Tyler!" I screamed. My footsteps pounded on the paved stones.

Someone passed me. I saw only my son bobbing eerily on the pool's suddenly choppy surface.

Tyler was floating in the deep end, facedown. Every horrible scenario flashed through my mind. *Oh, dear God. You already took my husband. Please, not my son.*

I jumped in and pushed through the warm water, but I wasn't the best swimmer. My clothes and tennis shoes weighed me down. Before I could reach him, Tyler was lifted out of the water. A pair of strong arms pulled me up.

"Lee," I said. I wiped the pool water off my face and whirled frantically.

"Ian has him." Lee's voice cracked, and his attention shifted. "Bridget, come out of the water, sweetheart."

Bridget scrunched her eyebrows to the center, concerned, her eyes on Tyler and Ian.

My sister pulled me into her shaky arms. "He's okay, Abby. Ty is okay."

He's okay.

My galloping heart slowed, but I had to see for myself.

"I'll get some towels," Kate said.

I got down on my knees, watching Ian assess Tyler. Tyler was sitting up, crossed-legged, wet, and shaking from the cold. But Ian wasn't performing CPR. Tyler wasn't coughing up water. Confused, but perfectly fine.

I was just as flabbergasted.

"I'm sorry, but I don't know what I did." Tyler glanced between all the adults. "Why did you pull me out of the water, Ian?"

"Ty, what were you doing?" I stood behind Ian, trembling from the cold. I tried to hold in my panic, even though all I wanted to do was yell at him for giving me the scare of my life, and then I wanted to hold him and never let him go.

"I was practicing floating and holding my breath. I wasn't jumping. I promise. Am I in trouble?"

My control nearly broke at that point. My adrenaline had finally settled, and relieved tears pricked my eyes. I blew out a lung full of air. Kate placed a towel around Tyler and handed two to Ian and me.

"No, honey." I stroked his cheek with my trembling hand. "I'm sorry. This is my fault. I thought … I thought …"

I didn't want to say it. I didn't want to worry him. He might freak out, or maybe I would if I said the words aloud. *I thought you drowned. I thought you were taken from me like your father.*

"You scared your mom, that's all." Ian wrapped the towel tighter around Tyler. "How about you and Bridget go get some ice cream inside the house? Then we can play *Buccaneers versus Skeletons* on the big screen. What do you say?"

Tyler's eyes rounded, replacing the annoyed, scared expression. "You play?"

"Aye, mate. Who do you think taught Lee? I beat his score."

"What?" Lee joined the teasing, his hands anchored on Bridget's shoulders. "Game on."

"Tyler, we have your favorite—chocolate chip ice cream," Bridget said. "Let's go and set the game up."

"We'll come with you." Kate tugged Lee toward the house, giving me space.

And just like that, everything was back to normal … except for me.

Oh, my heart. What was I thinking? What had I been doing, looking away while my child was swimming? I needed to be a better mother because I had to be good enough to make up for the parent he was missing. Later, at home, I would speak to Tyler about his position in the pool, how that might look to others, and why I had practically jumped on him.

I shouldn't have played ping-pong. I shouldn't have shared my time with Ian. A punishment and a warning. A reminder that I needed to put my child first above all.

"Abby. Ty is fine." Ian came closer, extending his arms for a hug, an effort to comfort me. He looked concerned, his towel around his shoulders.

But I didn't want that comfort. Didn't need it from him. I stepped back, keeping my distance. I looked away, no longer enticed. It wasn't his fault, but a part of me blamed him. Mostly I blamed myself.

I shivered and hugged the towel around me. "I appreciate your help. I'm going to get Tyler's clothes, and I need to change, too." My voice might have come out flat, but I could blame it on the soggy clothes clinging to my body.

I walked around Ian without a glance, grabbed the duffel bag, and headed inside.

Chapter Seven — Safe at Home

I knew I was overreacting, and I didn't mean to be rude to Ian. After all, he'd rushed ahead and pulled Tyler out of the water. I was grateful—but also mad at myself for being distracted. Watching over Tyler at the pool was my responsibility.

I didn't have to watch him like I had when he was younger, but kids his age still drowned. Freak accidents could happen.

After I changed, I joined everyone in the living room and watched the game on the large screen. Pirates with scarves tied around their heads and waving swords ran across the ship's deck to fight the sword-wielding skeletons. The clanking of weapons echoed through the indoor house speakers surrounding us. I felt like I was watching a movie in a theater.

The skeletons jumped aboard from rafts on a rocky ocean and pushed the treasure chest onto it. The lifelike pirates had to slay the skeletons before taking their wealth, on this level. The roguish captain, who had deep-set, dark eyes that gave the illusion he was wearing eyeliner, reminded me of Ian.

After a few rounds of *Buccaneers versus Skeletons*, I told everyone I was tired. Tyler wasn't happy we left first, but it was time to go home, anyway. I didn't want to overstay my welcome.

In the car, I explained to Tyler why I had jumped in the pool and why Ian had pulled him out. After Tyler washed up, I tucked him in bed and then grabbed a book I had left on the kitchen counter.

I needed something to help me relax and take my mind off the lingering guilt of being a terrible mother. Okay, so I wasn't *so* terrible. I told myself to stop dwelling on what could have been, but the memory of that moment, when I'd thought I'd lost my son, lingered. I never wanted to feel that agony again.

I snuggled under the covers and buttoned the top of my cotton pajama top. Without Steve, the queen-sized bed seemed too big.

Before I flipped my romance novel open, I looked over at the framed photo of Steve and me on the bedside table, next to my cell phone and the angel winged-shaped seashell I'd found on the beach.

THE SEASHELL OF 'OHANA

It was one of my favorite pictures of the two of us. We'd been in college. Steve had his arm draped around my shoulder as we exchanged loving glances. We had gone out that day with our friends to celebrate his birthday, and one of them had snapped the photo when we hadn't been paying attention to anything but each other.

Steve's hair had been slightly longer, then, making him look more like a surfer than a serious business student. One of the reasons why I'd been drawn to him. I tended to find the naughty boy type interesting, probably because I was more of a Mary Jane.

I smiled at the memory. Would Steve and I have gotten married so soon if I hadn't gotten pregnant? A year later, Tyler had been an infant, and Steve had been hired for a position in New York. A week after that, I'd gotten a job at a gallery in New York. We had been young, with great careers. Life had been so good.

Tap, tap came from my bedroom window. I jerked, my heart thundering. *What in the world?* Maybe a branch hit the glass? A bird? I ignored it.

Another tap, and another. It sounded like something was hitting the glass.

I jumped out of bed and padded barefoot to the window. I pulled down the plastic blind carefully with my index finger and snuck a peek. The pale crescent moon beamed brighter than the dim, yellow streetlamp. The night was so quiet and peaceful, I wondered if I had imagined the sound.

I jerked back when something whacked the glass in front of my face. That was when I saw my intruder. Kate stood between the white plumeria tree and a clump of pampas grass with a handful of pebbles, her right arm behind her, ready to throw again. I yanked up the blinds and opened the window. A gush of cool air greeted me, and I shivered.

"Hey! What are you doing?" I whispered sharply.

"Getting your attention."

I frowned. "Have you heard of knocking?"

"I didn't want to wake up Ty. And I didn't bring my key."

"Have you heard of a cell phone?"

Kate crossed her arms, defiant. "It went straight to your voicemail."

"It's a sign, Kate. It's like midnight, you know."

"I know. Let me in?" Kate walked away, in the direction of the porch.

"No," I said, a bit too loud, before she had made it past the lawn.

She stopped and whirled with an incredulous look. "What?"

"You heard me."

"Abby." She whined when she didn't get her way. "Come on, let me in."

I leaned closer, my nose almost pressed to the screen. "I don't need you to come for a pity party. I'm fine. Go back to Lee. He must think I'm insecure."

"He doesn't know I'm here."

I didn't buy her story. She was always at his place during the weekend. My sister, with a giant heart, a heart too big to fit in her chest, had left Lee to come be with me. I appreciated her looking after me, but now I felt guilty. I didn't need my baby sister. I just needed time.

"Kate, I'm fine." I used my motherly voice. "I'm going to sleep now. Go home."

"No."

"No?"

"Either let me in, or I'm going to stand here all night."

"Fine, then stand there," I said coolly.

Her eyes widened, and her lips moved, the way they did when she cursed under her breath. I closed the window and went back to bed. I assumed she'd gone home, but a pebble hit my window.

Not again. So stubborn.

A second pebble cracked against the glass. Again, I ignored her, but more kept coming. Damn, that girl could be persistent.

I huffed a breath and opened the window. "I told you to go home," I snapped.

"No, you told me to stand here all night. I'm going to keep doing this until you let me in. It's cold." She shivered, rubbing her arms.

Kate wore a pair of jeans and a T-shirt. She should be fine. It wasn't *that* cold, but I caved anyway. Little sisters always knew how to get their way.

"Fine." I stormed to the door and let her in.

Kate placed her sandals on the shoe rack and followed me to my bedroom. I flopped onto the bed, yanked the covers up, and fell back onto my pillow with an exaggerated sigh.

"I told you I was going to bed. See, I'm in bed. Now leave me alone." I closed my eyes and rolled to face the wall.

Footsteps shuffled to my closet, then my comforter shifted, and my sister tucked herself next to me. I flipped on my side to look at her, flabbergasted. She had changed into my pajamas.

"What are you doing?" I asked.

She lay on her side, her eyes level with mine, bright and gleaming in the moonlight pouring between the open blinds. I had forgotten to close them.

She was too chirpy for this time of night. But her soft expression made me feel horrible for trying to chase her away. I should be nicer to her.

Kate gave me a beautiful smile, all innocent and loving. "I wanted to be sure you were okay, that's all. And I want to be with you. I need my sister."

I flicked her forehead. "No, you don't."

"Ouch." She waved my hand away.

Silence fell between us. I closed my eyes, inhaled a deep breath, then opened my eyes again. How had my younger sister, who always needed me, become the stronger one?

"Thank you for checking up on me," I said. "It's sweet of you, but as you can see, I'm fine."

She bobbed a shoulder and adjusted the pillow to get comfortable. "So you say. I want you to know that you did nothing wrong. We were all watching the kids. If I had thought he …" She couldn't say it. "Well, I would have freaked out, too. I mean, we all were frantic until Ian pulled him out of the water and we could see he was fine. I know how you think, Abby. You weren't punished for having fun. Don't do this to yourself."

"Having a child is a huge responsibility. And being a single mom is hard." My voice cracked, and tears pooled in my eyes. "I'm a mom and a dad. I should have been watching him. What if … I can't lose him, too."

"I know, but it didn't happen. Tyler gave us a scare." She rolled her eyes and puffed out her cheeks with a frustrated huff. "I don't ever want to know what could have been." She squeezed me. "Do you remember when I told you about the time Bridget fell in the waterfall?"

I nodded and wiped away tears with my knuckles.

"Lee and I were right there. We watched her, but one second she was there and the next she wasn't. Thank God she'd had a few swimming lessons and her survival instincts kicked in. You've been amazing, raising Ty. You're teaching him and giving him tools to become independent. I'm not a mom, so I may be overstepping, especially with no experience raising a child, but I just want you to know that you're doing awesome."

She flashed her teeth in a huge, dorky grin, making me break into a sharp laugh.

"You need to give yourself more credit. You've helped me with Ty the past few years, and you're also like a mother to Bridget. You do know what you're talking about, and I value your opinion."

She lowered her eyelashes and offered a smile. "Do you remember what Mom and Dad used to tell us?"

"Of course, how could I forget?" I deepened my voice to sound like my father. "'Girls, I can provide you with the tools, but you'll have to be the one who knows how and when to use them.'"

"When we were young, we did more for ourselves." Kate held up a finger. "Like walk to school, make our lunch, and you had to take care of me after school until Mom came home. But we treat our kids like they're going to break if we don't do everything for them. It's a different generation for sure."

"Maybe we're making up for what our parents didn't do for us. Or maybe we know more." I threw up a hand in frustration. "The internet and social media gave us a reality check. We used to play outside until dark, but there's no way I would allow Ty to do that. I would worry too much, wonder who's trying to kidnap him."

Kate turned onto her back and peered at the ceiling. "Lee and I never allow Bridget out of our sight when we go out. I don't even let her use the restroom alone at the restaurants. Sometimes I wonder if we're too overbearing, but I'd rather her be safe than for me to be sorry."

I yawned and turned to my back, matching Kate. "Was I rude to Ian when we went inside the house?"

"No, but were you trying to be?" She sounded hesitant.

"No, of course not. I was just ..."

She stretched her arm to the ceiling. "You were less talkative, and that's understandable after the scare. But I have to say, you two were so cute when we were playing ping-pong."

"I'm not quite sure how to act around him. It's been so long since I've had a male friend."

"Just be yourself." Kate released a long yawn and snuggled onto her side to face me again.

"I guess. But sometimes I don't know who I am anymore."

Before Steve, I had been independent and focused. A go-getter. Steve and I had been a team, and our routine had been perfect until he'd gotten sick.

After Steve had died, life had become a rat race, and I ran all the time without a clear vision of where I was going. And I was too nervous about being back in the dating world anytime soon. I might never be ready. My son was safe and healthy, and that was all that mattered.

"You know who you are, Abby," my sister said with conviction. "You're one of the strongest women I know. You just need time to heal. I'm not trying to push Ian on you. If the chemistry is there, then great. When you're ready to let Steve go, you'll find love again."

I glanced at the photo of Steve and me. The streetlight hit perfectly across his face, and to me, he looked like an angel. Tyler's angel, and mine, watching over us from above.

His smile in the photo, the adoration on his face, made me heartsick. My composure ripped at the seams. The thought of moving on without Steve, I couldn't ... wouldn't.

"I miss him so much, Kate." My voice cracked, and I turned on my side. "There are days, too many of them, when I don't think I can go on."

"Oh, Abby." My sister draped her arm around me. "I miss him, too. He's looking down from Heaven, and he's so proud of you. Proud of your success. Proud of you for raising Ty alone. Proud of you for being strong."

"I'm so glad you're here." I let the tears fall onto my pillow. I didn't want my sister to see me like this, but she was the only person I'd allow myself to be vulnerable around.

Kate patted my shoulder in a steady rhythm, like a mother to a child. "I've never noticed that seashell by Steve's photo. Did you just put that there?"

I wiped my tears. "I went to the beach by myself on Steve's death anniversary. I was talking to him, and this seashell floated to me from the sea. I know it sounds crazy, but it's a gift from him to me. See how it looks like an angel's wings?"

I let out an odd sound between crying and laughing.

Kate reached over and touched the snow-white shell. "Now it's my turn to sound crazy, but you know how I'm all about fate and stuff. I believe in signs, and maybe someone is trying to communicate with you. Tune into it. It might help you with whatever is troubling you. And, Abby, I don't know much about shells, but I know for sure that one is called an angel wing." She bit her bottom lip. "Maybe Steve is trying to send you a message."

Chapter Eight — 'Ohana

"Hello, sweetheart." Steve's voice was jubilant.

Was I dreaming? I had to be.

I rolled to my side and rubbed my eyes. Steve was lying next to me, his face mashed into the pillow. He wore the red and green checkered PJs I had bought for all three of us the Christmas before he'd passed. Tyler had been one year old then, and we had taken a picture, a photo I'd cherished.

I stared at his face—his thick eyebrows, sharp nose, one dimple on his left cheek, and those stunning green eyes. I had hoped Tyler would inherit Steve's eye color, but he had gotten mine instead.

"Abby." Steve grinned. Plump cheeks and healthy skin replaced the pale, sunken face that pancreatic cancer had left him with. It had stolen so much from him and from all of us.

A divine light engulfed him. He looked content and peaceful in our bed, where he belonged. I knew I was dreaming, but I reached for him anyway. I wanted to hold him and keep him with me as long as I could, but my arms swiped at empty space.

It had been a while since I'd dreamed of him. This one felt too real, especially when he said my name. Maybe his death had been the dream—a nightmare—and when I awoke, he would be sleeping next to me. But he began to fade.

"Steve. Stay. Don't leave me." My voice rose in desperation, and I reached out for him again.

"Be happy, sweetheart."

"Abby? Abby." Not Steve's voice.

A hand gripped my shoulder, shaking gently. "Abby. Abby."

I flashed my eyes open to see my sister's concerned face inches from mine. "Kate?"

"Sorry. You were dreaming. What were you dreaming about?"

I parted my lips to tell her, but then I didn't. As simple as the dream was, it had been intimate and real. I wanted to keep it to myself.

"I can't remember." I sat up and ran a hand through my hair, feeling dazed. I needed a moment to get my bearings.

Footsteps pounded across the hall. A crack in the door opened wider, and Tyler pushed through.

"I heard voices." He squinted in confusion. "Auntie Kate?" He vaulted onto the bed and plopped between Kate and me. "What are you doing here?"

Kate squeezed him and kissed his cheek with an exaggerated plop. "Muah. I spent the night."

"You did?" Tyler crawled backward to the edge of the bed, landed on the hardwood floor with a thud, and straightened his pirate pajama top.

"Hey, where's my good morning hug and my kiss?" I crossed my arms and pouted.

He blinked and pointed at the seashell. "Wow. That's a new seashell. That one is special. 'Ohana. Nobody gets left behind or forgotten. That's a quote from *Lilo and Stitch* movie. When did you get that, Mom?"

"'Ohana?" I said, ignoring his question. He didn't need to know his mother had gone to the beach alone.

Kate slid off the bed and straightened her side of the blanket. "Lee told me 'ohana means family, but not necessary by blood. The people are bound together by compassion, loyalty, and love for each other. To be someone's 'ohana is a great honor. We came to earth to be together and will continue to do so after this life. Nobody gets left behind or forgotten. It is the spirit of 'ohana."

"I love that," I said softly.

Tyler tugged the blanket to get my attention. "I'm hungry. Mom, can I have pancakes for breakfast?"

"Of course you can."

After Tyler hugged me, he ran out of my room, and Kate chased after him. I grabbed my cell and strolled to the kitchen, still wearing my PJs. While I whipped up pancake batter and poured the first beige puddle into a sizzling frying pan, Kate showed Tyler pictures on her phone.

Because of the bond they shared, I had appointed Kate to be his guardian if something were to happen to me. Morbid thought, but it had to be done. After Steve had passed, I'd remembered every day that life was fleeting.

"Breakfast is ready." I flipped the last pancake onto a plate.

Kate poured coffee for both of us and juice for Tyler. Tyler pulled out the utensils and napkins and set them out on the table—his responsibility. Now that he was old enough to understand the value of money, I gave him a monthly allowance for helping around the house.

I placed the plates on the table and eased into a chair across from Kate. The white stoneware with blue orchids had been wedding gifts from one of my friends. I used these plates daily, but dreaming about Steve last night had me nearly in tears again. Some days, memory took hold more powerfully than others.

The first bittersweet taste of coffee hit my tongue, and my shoulders relaxed. "Kate, do you have plans today?"

"What did you have in mind?" She paused, her knife embedded in the stack of pancakes.

Her hesitation made me cautious. I didn't want her to feel like she had to spend time with me, especially after last night.

I bored my gaze into her. "If you have plans, don't change them."

"I don't." She turned to Tyler and smiled.

She avoided my eyes. I decided not to argue about it and enjoy her company. It seemed so rare, these days outside of work.

I swallowed a bite of syrup-drenched pancake and wiped my mouth with a paper napkin. "I was thinking we could drive up the North Shore to Hanalei. I know a place where they catch live seafood and serve it to you. It's a beautiful day and—"

"Perfect," Kate said before I could finish, and drank her coffee.

I arched my eyebrow. "Do you want to invite Lee and Bridget?" I asked to be polite.

"Not this time. Besides, it's been a while since the three of us did something together."

"Are you sure?" She hated when I second-guessed her, but I still suspected she was breaking plans to hang out with us.

"Yes, I'm sure," Kate pressed, a hint of annoyance in her tone. "But I'd like to go to my place and change first."

"Of course. Or you can borrow something of mine."

Tyler glanced between me and Kate, his grin hesitant at first and then growing. I knew he missed his aunt living with us, and he must be happy.

A flash of light on the table caught my attention. I hadn't checked my cell phone yet. A text had come from an unknown caller. I was going to dismiss it, but Kate asked, "Who is it?"

I clicked on it and read it out loud, assuming we'd get a laugh about a wrong number. "'Good morning. Just checking up on you. Last night was …'" I skipped a few words and stuttered to a stop. My cheeks warmed, and my voice hitched. "Oh, it's from Jane."

Kate gave me a suspicious sidelong glance. She'd caught on that I didn't want to say someone's name in front of Tyler. I didn't want my son to get the wrong impression of Ian and me. Not that there was anything between us besides friendship.

"Well, let's finish up and get going, right, Ty?" Kate slapped the table and stood, drawing his attention.

"I'm done." He stuffed in the last bite of pancake.

Kate cradled the coffee mug and took a sip. "Maybe you should reply." She gave me a wicked smile over the rim of her cup. "Let *Jane* know you're fine. Don't keep her waiting. It's rude."

I waved a hand like I was shooing away a fly and swiped the phone.

> **Abby:** Good morning. Thank you for your concern. Tyler and I are fine.

Maybe I should take out Tyler's name. I tried again.

> **Abby:** Good morning. Thank you for your concern. I'm fine. How are you? Kate came over last night and ...

I groaned. Why was I putting so much effort into one simple text? He'd asked me one question. Just answer.

Delete. Delete. Delete. Keep it simple.

> **Abby:** Good morning. Thank you for your concern. I'm fine.

I wasn't expecting a reply, so I got out of my seat, but Kate and Tyler had already put their plates in the sink. How long was I sitting here?

My heartbeat kicked up when the telltale blinking dots appeared. I sat back down.

> **Ian:** What are you doing today?

My fingers flew over the keys.

> **Abby:** Kate is spending the day with Ty and me.

> **Ian:** Lucky her.

I smiled and tapped out a message without a thought—and regretted the words as soon as I hit send.

Abby: Maybe next time, it' ll be your turn.

Oh dear God. What wild spirit had possessed my fingers?

"Kate," I practically screamed her name, swelling with panic. "Kate. Come here quick." I stood by the table, frozen and staring at my phone in horror.

Kate came rushing out of Tyler's room. "What? What happened?"

"How do I delete something I just sent?"

She extended her hand, palm up. "Give it to me. I'll see what I can do."

I put my phone behind my back. "No, just tell me. I can do it."

She crossed her arms and glared. "You mean you've never had to delete something you sent before?"

I shook my head. The only people I texted with were Kate, Stella, and a few of my friends. I'd never texted anyone something I regretted. Besides the basic things on my computer and the cell phone, I sucked at technology and had relied on Steve, so this was new territory.

"What do you want to hide from me?" She perked her lips, suppressing a smile.

"I'm not hiding anything." I frowned.

"Then give me the phone. The longer you wait, the more likely he's already read it."

My stomach twisted. I was wasting time, and it was probably too late.

"Here." I bit my bottom lip as I handed it to her.

She waggled her eyebrows, and her tone went all chirpy. "'Maybe next time it'll be your turn.' Good one, Abby."

"Hush. Did you do it?" I whispered sharply. I didn't want Tyler to hear our conversation.

She gave me my phone back and looked at me as if she had given me a death sentence. I thought that when she snickered, she was joking, but then she said, "I would have, but he's texting you back. So it's best you just leave it alone."

"Crap." I swiped to read it.

Ian: I'm counting on it.

My face burned. I had flirted with him, and he had reciprocated. Another time, and in other circumstances, I would have been enthralled, but I didn't want to lead him on. Things could get awkward. And he was like a brother to Lee, so that could upset my small social circle.

I cleared my throat, mortified, while my sister stood there gawking at me as if I was some kind of novelty.

"Are we going to stand here all day? Let's get going. Can you get Ty?" I grabbed my purse from the kitchen counter and headed in the direction of the garage.

"Abby. You might want to change out of your pajamas first." Kate burst into a laugh.

I halted by the door, then held my head up and marched toward my room, passing Kate without looking at her. My neck seared, but behind the door, I let myself giggle.

Chapter Nine — Hanalei

I veered the minivan onto the Kaumualii Highway, then to Highway 529, Maluhia Road, also known as the Tunnel of Trees—one of my favorite places on Kauai. That stretch of road always brought me peace.

A beautiful canopy of eucalyptus trees lined the road for a mile like leafy sentinels. Sunlight spilled through the cracks between the gray, arching branches and crisscrossed the pavement in golden streaks. We turned off to another highway and drove on for another hour.

No clouds graced us once we arrived, only a blanket of blue sky over a gentle stream, the palm trees, and thickets surrounding a lake. I banked right onto a small street at the sign with *Catch and Eat* carved on a wooden board. The minivan tilted like a seesaw as I slowed over the pebbled road and parked.

"Leave your purse in the car," I said to Kate, and looked over my shoulder to Tyler. "Watch out for the person getting in his car on your side."

After I stepped out, I grabbed two sunhats and my purse from the back of the van. I took a moment to close my eyes and inhale a deep breath, bathing in the sun. I loved coming to this side of Kauai.

I'd left my stress, worries, and responsibility in Poipu. There are no thoughts of painting deadlines or bills to pay or rushing Tyler to school. No thinking at all. Just a state of pure bliss and shutting the door on adulthood. Even the air felt lighter and fresher. The breeze curled around me in welcome.

"Where are we?" Kate's sandals crunched on the gravel walkway.

I tossed one of my straw sunhats to Kate and put on mine. Tyler squeezed between us as we meandered toward a small restaurant that looked like a cozy two-story house painted aqua blue.

"My friend brought me here last year." I'd meant to bring Tyler and Kate for a while, but time had slipped by. "They mostly serve to the locals, but get a few tourists. It's not on the map, so you have to hear about it through word of mouth."

"Shiver me timbers," Tyler exclaimed.

"You get to catch your own fish, and they'll cook it for you," I said. "Kate, I'll take care of the order."

I passed a few customers already seated on wooden benches and entered the house. After paying for three meals, I followed a concrete path to where Tyler and Kate stood behind the fence in the watching area. A family of four was fishing.

Colorful pebbles scattered on the path caught Tyler's eye. He wandered over and bent down, trailing his fingertips over them. He stood and looked around, restless, inching closer to the wooden walkway that led to the water.

"Hey Ty, stand next to your aunt," I called.

The blue sky, the sparkling water, and the vivid green of a cluster of trees made a perfect backdrop. I took pictures of Tyler and Kate with my phone, then Tyler by himself. And a selfie with the three of us.

"Is it our turn yet?" Tyler slumped his shoulders and let his head fall back, his voice heavy and low with an edge of whine seeping in.

I opened my mouth to answer, but a shadow loomed over us. A tall young man wearing jeans and a Catch and Eat T-shirt offered a wide grin, teeth gleaming in his well-tanned face. A white apron was tied around his slim waist. I recognized him.

"Abby?"

Justin owned a couple of restaurants and occasionally helped his parents at Catch and Eat when they went on vacation. I'd met him last year when he'd served my friend and me and then ran into him again at one of his upscale restaurants in Poipu. He had asked me out, but I had turned him down.

"Hello, Justin." I offered an affable smile.

"How have you been?" He planted a quick kiss on my cheek and pulled back, looking between Kate and Tyler.

I adjusted my hat, which almost blew away in a sudden breeze. "Justin, this is my sister Kate and my son, Tyler."

"Oh." He fixed his hazel eyes on Tyler, surprised.

He must be glad I'd turned him down. Most single men don't want to date someone who already has a child. Since I'd had no intention of saying yes, I hadn't felt the need to mention my single-mom status.

Justin turned to Kate, shook her hand, and gave Tyler a high five. "So, are you ready to catch your own fish?" he asked Tyler.

"Yeah!" Tyler whooped and punched the air.

Justin directed us onto the long walkway that extended over the lake. Our footsteps clomped on the wooden boards. Once we got to the end, he handed each of us a fishing rod, Tyler getting a smaller one. Then he worked a small, silvery baitfish onto each hook. I had to look away, but Tyler watched avidly.

Justin leaned over behind Tyler and helped him hold the rod. They both pulled their arms back and tossed the line.

"Good throw, Ty." Justin let go of the rod. "You wait here and keep an eye on that line."

"Look, Mom. I'm fishing."

I snapped pictures of Tyler smiling. He looked so proud, staring directly at the phone for only a second before concentrating on the water. Justin helped Kate get her line in the water, then me. I tried not to flinch when his chest brushed my arm.

Before long, one pole and then another bent with the weight of hungry fish. Justin helped Ty reel in his catch, then removed the wriggling fish from the hook. Once we'd all hooked our supper, Justin took the bucket with our fish inside the house. The cook would steam them while we waited.

I placed my purse and my phone on the edge of the table and sat on a bench seat that reminded me of school lunch tables.

"How do you know him?" Kate sat in front of me at the well-worn wooden table.

I lowered my voice so only she could hear. "It's a long story, but he asked me out last year." I took a quick peek at Tyler on the other side of Kate. He was busy with my phone.

My sister followed my gaze and then nodded. If I wasn't ready to date Ian now, I certainly wouldn't have dated Justin then.

A waitress set the plates down, the fish we had caught nestled beside sides of shrimp and rice pilaf. She unloaded two glasses of iced tea and a water bottle for Tyler from the tray, then scurried back to the kitchen.

Kate scooped up a small portion of her fish, dipped it in the plastic sauce container, and slid the bite into her mouth. "This is really good. I'm going to have to bring Lee and Bridget here."

Tyler said with a mouthful of rice, "Can we come again? This was so much fun. Maybe Ian can come, too."

Kate and I exchanged a shocked glance. I didn't know what to say. Tyler probably thought of Ian as part of the gang, Lee's buddy. His best friend was a girl, so he wouldn't jump to romance. I hoped.

I ignored his comment. Surely I was overreacting.

"How about we get some shaved ice after lunch?" I hastily dug into my fish as Tyler's face lit up.

A successful distraction. While we ate, Tyler chattered about all the flavors, listing his favorites and changing his mind over and over again on which he would get.

My phone beeped.

"Here you go, Mom." Tyler set my cell in front of me.

When I picked it up, my face heated despite the perfect temperature. It was a good thing he hadn't looked at the caller ID. Ian had texted me.

"Who's it from?" My sister took a long sip of her tea.

Tyler gnawed on a shrimp and turned around on the bench to watch other families fishing.

I leaned in and lowered my voice. "It's Ian. He wants to know what I'm doing."

Kate beamed a smile and waggled her eyebrows. She returned to her meal with a nonchalant smirk, which drove me crazy wondering what she thought. Instead of texting back, I sent him a photo of Tyler and Kate with their fish, then showed Kate the picture.

Kate set down her iced tea and licked her lips. "He asked what *you* were doing, not us." She snorted. "I'm sure he's going to love seeing Ty and me."

"I don't want to send a picture of myself. It's weird." I forked up a mound of fish and rice.

Kate angled her sunhat so the late sun fell across her face. "It's fine to send a picture of yourself. You're friends. He knows about Steve, and he probably thinks of you as family, as he does me."

I pushed a shrimp around my plate and begrudgingly agreed. The friendly kiss and the chat were simple acts of friendship. And, like always, I was over thinking and being paranoid. I needed to give myself a break.

It had been ages since I'd had a male friend, but Ian wasn't just some guy. He was Lee's friend and was safe to let into our lives. Cautiously. I glanced at my phone when it beeped.

> Ian: Looks like the three of you are having
> fun, but where are you in the picture?

I let out a small laugh and sent a picture of the selfie I had taken of the three of us.

The message came fast.

> Ian: Better. Enjoy, and drive safe coming
> back home.

I debated asking him what he was doing, but I let it go when the dots rolled. Another text came through.

Ian: I'm stopping by with a client tomorrow.

"Abby." A hand waved in front of my face.

I peered up, squinting into the sunlight. "Justin. Oh, sorry." I put my phone facedown.

"Looks like you were deep in thought. Anyway, how was everything?" He gestured to the empty table.

Kate had cleaned up while I had been glued to the phone, debating what to say and what picture to send. So much thought was put into a simple text. *Good grief.*

"It was perfect," I said. "How long are your parents on vacation?"

Justin's expression turned somber. "My dad had a stroke. I'll need to hire someone to manage this place, or I'm going to have to sell it."

"I'm so sorry, Justin. Will he be okay? How bad is it?"

"It happened a couple of days ago. We'll know more soon."

I nodded, my lips pressed tight. "Please, give my love to your dad. He doesn't know me, but I wish him well. And I know his customers will miss him."

"Thanks. Anyway, I should get back inside. It was nice seeing you again."

I watched him walk away and wondered if I *would* ever see him again. His grief and worry were familiar to me, and reading those feelings in Justin's face reminded me of Steve. Life was so fleeting and sad, but there was also joy. I looked over to my son, my love, my happiness. He gave me a reason to wake up every morning.

"Let's go get some dessert, shall we?" I said, to lighten the oppressive mood.

"Aye, Captain. Shaved ice, here we come." Tyler licked his lips and tugged Kate out of her seat.

Chapter Ten — Back to Work

"**G**ood morning," Stella chirped when I pushed through the front door at the gallery the next morning.

The wind chimes tinkled, soothing and sweet to my ears.

"How was your weekend?" I headed to the table, swinging my purse off my arm. "Fun, I hope."

Stella blinked with surprise like I had spoken in another language. "Fi ... ne." She sounded unsure. "You sound happy."

I narrowed my eyes, confused. I greeted her the same way I did every day. Before I could say anything, Kate strolled in with her hips swaying, wearing her bubbly mood in a warm smile and bouncy step. Heels instead of flat sandals clicked on the floor.

Kate adjusted her shirt, a cute coral front-tie, and straightened her white linen pants. Instead of pulling her hair back into a ponytail, she had curled it. Soft makeup highlighted her eyes, cheeks, and lips. She looked stunning.

"You going to paint wearing that?" I poured myself a coffee and took a sip.

Kate waved at Stella and frowned at me. "I'm going to wear an apron, of course. Lee is taking me out to lunch. He's coming by with Ian."

As if Kate had dropped a bit of juicy gossip, Stella swirled her desk chair around and gave me a once-over.

"So that's why you look nice today," she said.

It took me a second to register what she was talking about. I glanced down at my attire: a white tank under a sky-blue wrap and jeans. I always glossed on a light lipstick, but today I'd also brushed on light cream and brown eyeshadow and accentuated my cheekbones with baby pink. Looking nice was part of the job.

"What do you mean? I'm dressed how I do every day."

"Umm-hmm." Stella furrowed her brow and turned back to the monitor. "Whatever you say."

Ugh. She was the absolute queen of the sarcastic tone.

Stella had thrown the same attitude toward Kate when she'd thought Kate had a thing for Lee. But my situation was different. Ian was bringing a potential client. I wanted to look professional and have a Hawaiian vibe, the way many clients expected. That was all.

Kate didn't say anything, but she curled her lips smugly as she strolled to the back room. My heels thudded faster than hers as I followed, my paper mug of coffee in my hand. I placed it on the table with my purse and went to the shelf.

Kate tied on a full-body painting apron and secured on her earbuds. Humming a tune, she sat on her stool and started mixing colors. After gathering supplies and putting on my apron, I took the standing easel beside her and picked up a brush.

I cracked up a few times while listening to her out-of-tune singing. If it was a song I knew, I sang softly with her. Sometimes, I wished I could be carefree like her, belt out the lyrics and not care if anyone listened.

I got busy, lost to my brushstrokes on the canvas. A clear, cylindrical vase sat on a table, with stalks of violet, white, and pink orchids—a classic still-life with nearly photo-realistic details. It was a commissioned painting from a local. The morning went quickly, and before I knew it, it was almost noon.

"Kate. Abby. You have company," Stella sang through the speakerphone.

Kate hurriedly took off her apron and tossed it on the chair. Before I had a chance to cap a tube of paint, she undid my apron, slipped it over my head, and tugged me out with her.

What were we, teenagers waiting for prom dates? But my heart hammered like a schoolgirl with a crush when I spotted Ian standing next to Lee at the front desk. He sported dark gray jeans and a white linen button-up. That devilish grin he produced when he saw me awakened hundreds of butterflies inside my chest.

Kate greeted Lee and Ian with a kiss and a hug, and I did the same. Ian smelled of mint and sea breeze.

Ian used to be a stockbroker, but he had taken his earnings and moved to real estate, investing in properties under Lee's management. They had even purchased land together, planning to build hotels. Ian hadn't shared this information with me. I'd gotten the scoop from Kate yesterday while we'd eaten shaved ice.

When I pulled away, I noted a woman standing behind him. She had her head down, fumbling for something inside her purse. She was

THE SEASHELL OF 'OHANA

beautiful, with shoulder-length red hair and a black dress that clung to her delicate curves. Her manicured nails sparkled, and so did her diamond earrings.

Her hazel eyes landed on me, and her smile vanished. Compared to this woman, I might as well have worn rags. I felt so small, and I wanted to melt into the tile floor.

"Abby, Kate, this is Kristina," Ian said.

The woman extended her hand like a princess to Kate first, then me. She gave me a half-shake, taking only four of my fingers.

"I've heard wonderful things about your gallery from Ian." Her voice was low and seductive, but she didn't sound genuine. "It's finally nice to meet you both."

I didn't know her, and already I didn't like her. She reminded me of the snooty girls I'd avoided in high school. Her shoulder brushed against Ian's arm as she sidled up to him as if he belonged to her. Maybe they were dating. Confused emotions erupted from me, jealousy foremost. I pushed back the resentment I had no right to feel.

Act professional.

Ian had every right to date who he wanted. But her? She seemed snooty and rude. I couldn't imagine him with someone like that. Why not? A handsome, wealthy bachelor has needs, and surely women threw themselves at him.

"The pleasure is mine," I said with as much pleasantry as I could muster. "Are you here to accompany Ian, or …?"

I met Ian's gaze for further explanation. I wasn't sure if she were the client he'd referenced in his text or if someone else was on their way. When Ian gave me a grin, she cleared her throat and spoke.

"Can you ship them? I'm interested in purchasing a few pieces for my new place in New York."

Kristina peered up on the wall in front of her. Her gaze drifted from one frame to another. She had asked the question without looking my way.

"I can," I said. "Come this way, please."

As Lee, Kate, and Ian chatted, I escorted Kristina around the gallery.

I waved a hand to one of my favorites. "This one is called *Tunnel of Trees*. It's a portrayal of the iconic one on Maluhia Road."

Kristina drew closer with her hand raised. Her fingertips almost grazed the surface, but she let her arm fall to her side. "This painting is so lifelike. I feel like I'm there. I love the play of light and shadow. What kind of trees are they?"

"Eucalyptus. My sister painted it." I looked over my shoulder at her.

The three of them faced Stella, and they seemed to be in a deep conversation. I wondered what they were talking about.

"And this one." I pointed to the adjacent frame. "*Wailua Falls*. Another of my favorites."

Kristina edged closer to the painting, examining a detail in the corner, then backed away. Oil paintings were meant to be looked at from a distance.

She scrunched her eyebrows then relaxed them. "I love how the artist captured the rainbow arching over the water. It's breathtaking. Did Kate paint that one as well?"

"No, I did," I said hesitantly.

It didn't matter how many years I'd been selling my work, but getting compliments had me flushing.

"Oh," she said with a hint of disdain. Her shoulders fell, and she backed away nonchalantly.

I clenched my teeth, ignoring her subtle snub, and moved on. I showed her blown-up photos of sea turtles, city lights in oil, waterfalls in acrylic, orchids done with watercolors, and other paintings.

Our gallery showcased a variety of work from almost exclusively Hawaii-based artists. Then I showed her some of Kate's amazing photographs, blown up to poster size, and raved about the sculptures by the window.

Kristina looked over her shoulder and pointed at the *Tunnel of Trees*. "Ian. What do you think, dear? Would it go well with the colors in my home?"

Dear? Did she just call him dear?

"What?" Ian looked at Kristina. He crinkled his brow and gave her a sidelong glance, looking confused. He'd heard his name and had been pulled away from the conversation.

She let out a sharp sigh. "Would this one go well with my house?"

"I haven't been to your new place. I have no idea." He returned to Lee and Kate.

Ian didn't sound rude, but Kristina turned away with a hiss, seemingly embarrassed. If she wanted me to think she and Ian were a happy couple, she hadn't gotten the result she'd hoped for.

Kristina frowned, her nose flaring, then gave me a wry smile when our eyes met. "There are so many. It's hard to decide." Her gaze went from one wall to the other, then to the shelf by the window. "I'm not a decorator, but I suppose if they don't match the color scheme in New York, they can go to my other property." Her words were soft and low, as if she was talking to herself.

Lucky for her. It must be nice to have the luxury to purchase anything she wanted. She could toss them aside if she didn't need them, and not worry about how much she had spent.

"If none of them are what you're looking for, then we can—"

"I have my mind made up." Her words cut through mine, sharp and demanding.

Never in the four years I'd owned the gallery had any client been rude to me. She was obviously used to getting her way.

"I would like this one and that one." She pointed to the *Tunnel of Trees* and a few others, all of them Kate's masterpieces. None of them were mine, not even the waterfall she seemed to have admired the most.

Maybe she didn't like me. I had to admit, I was a bit taken aback to see her, so it was possible I'd given her my bitchy face and made a bad impression. I hadn't meant to, but whatever.

She could have Ian or whichever paintings she liked. I wasn't the type to play games, and I certainly didn't have time for petty people.

"And I need them shipped to an address in New York immediately," she said, like she was ordering her assistant to make a lunch reservation.

I bit my bottom lip. *Be kind and just make the sale. You're almost done, and you'll never have to deal with her again.*

My sister joined us, looking at me warily. She must have heard Kristina's tone and sensed my irritation. Kate hiked an eyebrow, silently asking if I was okay. I rolled my eyes to reply. Then, with much effort, I gave Kristina a bright smile when we locked gazes.

As Kristina strutted over to Ian, I asked Stella to help me.

While Stella carefully unhooked the turtle painting off the wall, I dragged a stool next to the sofa. I planted my feet on top of the stool, like I had done countless times, and reached for the *Tunnel of Trees* painting.

I should have gotten a stepladder from the back. The legs wobbled when I stepped onto the stool. Something was caught under them, or perhaps it was an uneven surface. My weight shifted, throwing me off balance. My poor judgment would cost me.

The moment held an ominous sense of déjà vu. Ian had stopped my almost-fall at the market, but it wasn't going to happen again. In that frozen moment, the stool sliding backward, I prepared to make a fool out of myself. Maybe end up with a broken something or other. Instead of crash landing on my face, I ended in a pair of strong arms.

"Whoa. I got ya. You don't have to fall to get my attention, Abby. You already have it." Hot breath brushed against the side of my face when he brought me to my feet.

"Ian," I muttered at the crook of his neck. My lips touched his skin. Every inch of him was pressing against me. My skin flushed so hot, my ears burned.

Oh, God. How this must look. But I'd liked the warmth of him and the tightness of his strong arms around me. How I'd longed for that human touch, to be reminded what it felt like to be held by a man.

I pushed back slowly, afraid to meet his gaze, but there was no escaping the fact that I needed to thank him. Gorgeous brown eyes met mine. I lost my words, consumed by his touch and the way he looked at me. Confused? Longing? I had no idea. But his expression woke something alive in me.

"I-I ..."

A chair scraping across the floor came from my left. Our spell broke when someone cleared their throat. As I smoothed out my shirt and ran my fingers through my hair, trying not to look at anyone, Kristina clamped her fingers on Ian's arm and pried him away.

My sister came running, her chest heaving. "Are you okay?"

I put up a hand, a silent gesture to let her know I was fine. She understood and backed away.

Kristina let out a fake giggle. "Really, Ian. Always rushing to people's rescue. You should be more careful, Abby. Getting hurt in front of customers is no way to run a business."

She didn't raise her voice, but her snarky tone boomed like thunder. *Go walk the plank, wench.*

Tyler's silly pirate talk helped tamp down the rage that had so quickly consumed me that my hands shook. *Be nice. She's a customer. You don't want her spreading rumors.*

Imagining pushing her off the plank, I found my best smile and said, "Stella will ring you up."

"Of course." Stella's serious tone caught my attention. She, too, was standing, her fingers gripping the edge of her desk. "Will that be cash or credit?"

I wanted to hide in the backroom, both to escape my weird mix of feelings and to avoid saying anything I might regret. Ian had called her a client, and I had trouble believing he'd go for someone like her. If they had something more, I hoped he dumped her.

I'd had all types of customers, including demanding ones who wanted custom pieces. When I had been in New York, having to smile through tiny insults from snobby clients was the norm. But it was my gallery, and after what I'd lived through with Steve, my patience for people like her was low. This woman … this woman … she'd riled me up. I wished I could shake her, and I wasn't the violent type.

"It was nice to meet you, Kristina." I squared my shoulders and held up my chin. "I'll be in the back room if anyone needs me."

My flats gave a slap on the floor, the only sound in the room as I got the hell out of there. When I reached the door, I heard Ian tell Kristina he had to cancel their lunch. I allowed myself a small grin and only felt a tiny bit bad about it.

There was a small knock just as the door closed behind me.

Stella or Kate would have entered without knocking, so it had to be Ian. He must have dashed across the room, to have gotten to me so fast.

Chapter Eleven — Apology

I froze by the door at the first knock. I didn't want to see Ian. The day had started great. What had happened? When the second knock came, I cringed and opened the door. There was no way to avoid facing him. He knew I was inside. I had announced I would be in the back room, and there wasn't another exit.

Time to act like an adult, Abby.

Ian barged in and shut the door behind him. His wide eyes locked on mine, full of concern. He reached out to me but let his arms fall back to his sides.

"Abby, I'm so sorry." He sounded desperate, almost panicky. "I wouldn't have brought Kristina here if I'd known she'd ..." He shook his head. "To be honest, I'm surprised by how she treated you."

Because I felt guilty for wishing Kristina ill, a part of me had thought he had marched right over to tell me I had done something wrong.

"You don't need to apologize for her, Ian. She's your client."

His features contorted in a scowl as he paced from my easel to my desk, mumbling, "I thought ... I can't believe ... why would ..."

"Ian, what are you talking about?" I almost laughed. The calm, cool, collected man I knew was flustered and mumbling to himself.

My anger subsided, but not my pulse. His large, muscled form took up way too much room in the small workspace. And his confusion was adorable. I had to push away the image of him shoving everything off the desk with one swipe of his hand like the hunky love interest in a movie. I ordered myself to stop thinking about Ian yanking me into his arms and kissing me senselessly.

Ian halted in front of me and squinted. He looked like he had been at war with himself, but had made up his mind. For one slow heartbeat, I expected him to do everything I'd envisioned.

When our eyes locked, I couldn't look away. His beautiful, deep-set, dark eyes reeled me in. He would make a hot pirate, and I added a pirate hat to my mental image. What was I thinking?

Ian raked back his hair. "Kristina is my ex. We dated about a year ago."

"Oh." I might have squeaked.

Why would he date someone like ... but what did I know about him? Come to think of it, not much. I'd assumed he was an upstanding guy because he was Lee's friend.

"It's a long story, but please don't judge me. She was different, or I thought she was. We broke up when she revealed her true personality."

I leaned against the desk and crossed my arms.

"We didn't date long," Ian added. "I haven't spoken to her in months, but she reached out when she heard about my partnership with Lee. She's interested in investing in one of our properties in San Diego. I told her about your gallery. She knows many people, and I thought it would be good business for you. I also raved about you, how talented you are."

Heat snaked up my neck. "Thank you, but I think she wants you back."

Ian let out a sharp chuckle. "Maybe." He paused as if to gather his thoughts. "She obviously wanted to check out her competition."

I stiffened and retreated a step.

"I mean ..." He ran a hand down his face. "Because I've said nice things about you. She gets very jealous."

"Is she Lee's friend?" I asked.

He chuckled, rubbing the line of his jaw. "He can't stand her. He warned me about her, but I'm the type of guy who likes to give people the benefit of the doubt and look for the good in them."

Me too, and I like that about you.

"Anyway—" He cleared his throat, giving me puppy eyes, his lips turned downward. "I would like to make this up to you. Can I take you out to lunch?"

"I ... um ..." My mouth went dry. I shouldn't have to think about it. I had no plans.

"Kate and Lee will be there," he said. "It'll be fun. And I'll make Lee pay for lunch." He winked.

That wink. Dear God, that wink. He could probably convince me to do anything.

"Well, as long as Lee pays for lunch, then I'll come."

His eyes gleamed, and his smile grew wider. "After you." He pushed opened the door and said, "Lee, you're buying lunch."

I laughed at his mischievous spark, and I think I fell a tad more.

Ian drove the four of us to the Beach House Restaurant on Lawai Road in his sleek black Audi. I had been past the restaurant before, which was nestled on the beach, but never ventured in. When I stepped out of the car, a warm breeze tugged at my clothes. Hypnotic waves pulsed over the shore.

In the deeper water, boats sailed, and surfers rode the waves. Families gathered on the white sand, resting under broad umbrellas or setting out beach picnics.

Lee had called earlier to make a reservation. The waitress seated us near the back, where it was quieter. She brought us our drinks after we ordered, and left.

Lee rested his elbows on the table with his arms crossed. "So, Abby. Do you like my piña colada, or the restaurant's?"

I sipped my drink, savoring the cool sensation down my throat, and gave my lips an exaggerated smack. "I don't know, Lee. This one's pretty good."

Ian barked a laugh. "She can like both."

Kate kissed Lee's cheek. "Yours is *definitely* the best."

Kate got a big kiss on the lips for that, and Ian and I exchanged disgusted expressions, as if we were their kids. While we chatted away about the gallery and how Kate and I were swamped, our food arrived.

A waitress with a purple hibiscus flower in her hair set down a tray of small bites and a mound of vibrant greens and began serving portions onto our plates. "This is pumpkin ravioli. Szechuan stir-fry green beans. Omao arugula and goat cheese macadamia salad."

My mouth watered. These were just the appetizers.

My first bite of peppery arugula melded with the nutty crunch of macadamias. A tangy vinaigrette dressing with a hint of strawberry rounded out the blend of flavors.

"Who knew salad could be this good?" I said.

"We should have ordered everything on the menu since Lee's buying." Ian chuckled and took a bite of the green beans.

"Next time, I choose the restaurant, and you pay." Lee sipped his martini and scooped up a pumpkin ravioli.

Kate and I laughed. I loved their comfortable banter.

Shortly after, our lunch was served. I had ordered a grilled mahi sandwich with beach house pineapple tartar sauce.

"Mmmm, this sauce is amazing."

"It's one of my favorites." Ian chomped down on a giant Kobe beef hamburger. "Want a fry?" He placed a handful on my plate and said, "One of my clients, Mr. Romano, is having a special auction at his place at the end of the month. I have four tickets. Everyone in?"

Lee stole one of Ian's fries. "You know I am."

Kate said, "Sure. It sounds fun. How about you, Abby?" She twirled her fork around the jumbo shrimp on her seafood salad.

"I'll need to get Tyler a sitter. I can probably ask Stella. She's watched him before, and …" Warmth distracted me. Not a blush, but the warmth of another body close to mine. I stopped talking and shifted my gaze to Ian, whose thigh rested next to mine.

He had his elbow on the table and his chin on his fist, staring at me. His long, dark eyelashes lowered. He let his gaze linger on my mouth, then looked into my eyes with such intensity that heat blazed straight through to my bones. I snapped out of his lure, wrung my fingers on the cool glass, and took a fast sip of my drink to cool myself down.

Oh, Ian. You know exactly what you're doing. You're bad!

Lee wiped his mouth with a cloth napkin. "Mona can watch Ty."

Tyler was my responsibility, and I never wanted to impose on Lee or Mona.

"I insist," Lee said. "Tyler and Bridget can keep each other company, and she won't be so bored. Besides, I don't want you to worry about time. I want you to relax and enjoy yourself. And keep Ian out of my hair." He chuckled.

I snickered under my breath and took another bite of my fish sandwich. "Thank you, Lee. That's kind of you."

"What he means is …" Ian swallowed and pointed a fork at his friend. "You need to protect me from Lee. He's a bully."

Lee shrugged. "Don't you mean I need to save you from women like Kristina? I still can't believe you dated her. Speaking of which, I know Ian apologized, but I want to apologize, too, Abby. We were so busy talking we weren't paying attention to what she was saying. You were professional, and I appreciate that."

My cheeks, already flushed from the alcohol, felt hotter. It was sweet of Lee to bring it up, but unnecessary. These two men were such gentlemen. I was glad Kate had met a guy like Lee after her previous jerk of a boyfriend. And I appreciated Ian, too. Even without romance, he was a good man to have in my life.

"It's fine, Lee. Ian got down on his knees and begged for

forgiveness. I finally forgave him after he groveled and kissed my feet."

I wanted Ian to know that I wasn't all serious, though the joke didn't come out easy at first. It had been a while, but I still knew how to tease and flirt.

Lee almost dropped his glass, and Ian gawked at me with wide eyes.

"You evil, naughty, but sweet person." Ian raised an eyebrow. "I think I'm in love with you."

We shared a laugh. Even though we all knew Ian was joking, I shifted uncomfortably in my seat and picked up a french fry to avoid his eyes. Of course, he didn't mean that he loved me, but hearing it—those intimate words pricked at my heart. It almost stung worse as a joke.

Would I ever find love again without Steve? Maybe someday, but I needed to concentrate on my son.

Back at the gallery, I had to admit that I'd had a wonderful time. It was a great break in the mundane routine, and I was looking forward to the auction.

I picked up Tyler from school and brought him to the gallery. He whined, but I promised him tablet time if he'd help me tidy up. We had so many deadlines that I had no choice but to work late hours several nights a week. The gallery had become our second home.

We really needed to hire someone. Luckily, we already had several responses to our online "help wanted" ad. Stella would screen the candidates before the initial interview. I suspected she relished the chance to wield a little power, but we trusted her judgment.

Chapter Twelve — Sick Day

I dropped off Tyler at school and came back home to sleep. My head pounded, and drinking water didn't soothe the soreness in my throat. I blamed my fever on exhaustion from long hours at work—lack of sleep had opened up the door to whatever germs were circulating.

Great. This was just great. I had too many deadlines, and I couldn't afford to get sick. I had already messaged Kate and Stella to let them know I was going to be in late, but now I would have to tell them I wasn't coming in at all. Hopefully, I could fight this off with sleep and some medicine.

I reached my phone from the bedside table when it pinged with a text.

> Kate: Don't come in. Rest up. I'll pick up
> Tyler after school. Let me know if you need
> anything.

I gave her a heart emoji and plopped my head back to the pillow. I should have been more careful. My body had been shooting warning signals to slow down for days—eventually, I'd learn to pay attention.

Kate hardly ever got sick. I was the one who caught a cold every winter and attracted every virus that went around Tyler's school. In high school, she would sleep in my bed to try to catch my germs. It never worked.

Alone in the quiet, I thought about Steve and how we met in college.

I had been standing in line at a small café inside the USC campus, debating what to order from a list of soup specials, when the guy in front of me bumped into me.

I stumbled back and almost dropped my paper cup of coffee. The warm liquid sloshed through the lid hole, and a few drops landed on my hand. Good thing it had a cap. Even better that I had come after the rush hour. Aside from the clumsy guy in front of me, I was the only one in line.

"What the—" a deep voice said.

I peered up, muttering curses under my breath. Pretty green eyes met mine, and I put on the brakes. He sported jeans and an olive sweater, and the spark between us softened me instantly.

It was like a scene from a movie where two people just stood there, staring at each other, enchanted. No words were needed, just an instant connection. If there were such a thing as soulmates, he was mine, and I was his.

"Are you okay? Did I hurt you?" His abrupt, annoyed tone had softened to concern. "I'm so sorry. I tripped, and you caught my fall." His lips curled wickedly, and his eyes danced.

"I'm fine. But do you normally use small women to break your fall?"

He scoffed, but his grin widened. "Only the ones I find attractive. My name is Steve, by the way."

Nice one, Steve.

My cheeks warmed, and I offered a broad smile.

"My name is Abby." I puffed out a breath to push the strands that had fallen on my face.

Steve glanced down at my full hands—books in one, paper cup of coffee in the other—and tucked the wayward strand around my ears. "There. Now I can see your pretty eyes, Abby." He gestured to the cashier with his chin. "I think it's our turn to order. Whatever you're having, I'm paying. It's the least I can do for nearly running you over."

A little arrogant, but in a playful way. Normally, I would have politely turned him down, but I felt bold that day.

Live a little, my daring voice said.

I had taken a leap of faith. Steve and I had lunch, just the two of us as if the universe wanted us to be together. That lunch was followed by other carefree campus lunches and many more happy memories. What can compete with young love?

I yawned and slipped into a deep slumber.

"Sweetheart." Steve smiled.

Like the last time he appeared in my dreams, a white light engulfed him in a divine glow. We faced each other across the pillows, lying on our sides.

"Steve." I reached for him, but my arms swiped at empty space, and he began to fade. "Steve. Come back." The words echoed in my head.

My eyes fluttered open, and I gasped as if having been underwater. I kicked the blanket off me and sprawled on top of the covers, sweltering. Sweat beaded my forehead and chest. I swiped a hand across my face, then fanned my PJ top.

How long had I been asleep? What time was it?

I grabbed my cell. Any minute now, Kate would walk in the door with Tyler. I groaned and closed my eyes to welcome sleep once more, still feeling like I had been hit by a bus.

The door creaked and footsteps padded on the wooden floor. Whispering voices filtered through the ajar bedroom door.

"Mom. Are you asleep?" Tyler's voice was so low it was hardly audible.

"Ty. You can come in, but don't come too close." I pushed on the mattress to support my weight and sat up. I smiled weakly. "How was school?"

Tyler stood on the threshold. "Good. I have lots of homework. Are you sick like the last time?"

Years ago, I'd caught the flu and had been knocked out for a week. Kate had taken over mom duties, driving Tyler to school and taking care of me. Bless her heart for being the best sister. It seemed I'd inherited the weaker immune system.

"You don't have to worry. I just need a good sleep and I'll be good as new. What's your Auntie Kate doing? She picked you up, right?"

Kate would be marching through the door any minute to reprimand me for overworking. She was probably in the kitchen, but no sound came from any part of the house.

Tyler shifted on his feet. "Auntie Kate couldn't make it. She said something about interviews, and she'll explain later."

"Then who picked you up?" I scrubbed my face and yawned. Lee? Lee's driver? One of Tyler's friends?

A tall figure slid behind my son, shoving his hands inside the front pockets of his jeans. His smile was reserved, but bright enough to warm the room ... and me.

"Hello, Abby," Ian said with that cool, soothing voice that made me jolt.

My name came off a bit fun and flirty, like his grin. At least that was how I'd heard it.

"Ian?" He hadn't even crossed my mind.

"Kate called me. Lee was in a meeting. She couldn't get a hold of him, and I was free."

I pulled up the blanket to my chest. I wasn't wearing anything revealing, but him seeing me in my bedroom seemed intimate in a way I wasn't prepared for. And in my sick state, I wondered what I looked like. Crappy, I'd bet, with red-rimmed eyes and—oh God, my hair. It must be all over the place from tossing and turning.

"I appreciate your help. You probably have to go."

As the words spewed out of my mouth, the realization sank in— the house. I had been so busy the past week that I had neglected cleaning, even shoved the dirty dishes aside to wash later. I had never been so disorganized and messy. Even sick, I would typically still clean.

Ian rubbed Tyler's shoulders. "Actually, I stopped by Mama's Kitchen to pick up dinner and homemade chicken soup for you. I hope you don't mind that I invited myself for dinner, but I didn't know how sick you were."

So thoughtful of him. His presence somehow made me less tired and maybe even less sick. I twisted the top button on my lavender pajama top, ensuring it was in place before pushing up to sit higher in the bed.

"That's so sweet of you. Please stay for dinner, but I'm afraid I'm not going to be good company. And you'll have to excuse my messy home. I've been so busy at the gallery, I hardly had time for anything else."

He pressed his lips into a frown. "It's understandable. We all push to the breaking point. Anyway, if you need anything, let me know. While you rest up, I'll help Ty with his homework. Sound good, Ty?"

Tyler, who'd been patiently waiting, glancing back and forth between Ian and me, said, "You told me you were good in math, in the car. I need help, please."

"Yes, sir." He saluted Tyler. "And you, my queen." He turned to me. "You stay in bed and rest. And Master Ty, you come with me."

Tyler and I laughed.

Ian left my door ajar, and I could hear soft murmurs. Sometimes Tyler laughed, the sound like lovely music. As I wondered what they were talking about, I drifted in and out of sleep and finally into a deep slumber.

When I awoke, I felt much better. I put on a white robe and walked out. The moon had replaced the sun, and stars dotted the night sky. Lights were turned on in the kitchen and the family room.

I stepped carefully down the hall, quiet as a mouse so I wouldn't disturb them. To be honest, I wanted to see what they were doing.

My fairy godmother had swooped down and cleaned up the mess. Tyler's clothes were folded neatly inside the laundry basket. His toys and books were stacked back into their slots on a wooden cabinet. Dishes were washed, and the dry ones were put away. And the blanket and cushion pillows had been picked up and arranged tidily on the sofa.

Tyler and Ian were sitting at the dining table, and Tyler was reading aloud to Ian. Something he refused to do with me. Ian would ask him a question, then he would praise Tyler when he answered. Tyler's eyes beamed, round and bright like the moon in the window behind him.

The floor creaked when I took the next step. Like a thief in the night, I froze.

"Abby." Ian came around the table and stood between the family room and the kitchen. "You were sleeping, and I didn't want to wake you. You must be hungry. Let me heat your soup."

"Ian, I can do it. You don't need to take care of me." I fluttered my hands and dropped them back to my sides.

Ian ignored me as he placed a bowl in the microwave. Knowing he wouldn't cave, I pulled out a chair and sat next to Tyler.

"I'm done with homework." The book in Tyler's hand thumped on top of another book on the table. "Ian helped me with math, and we read together. Homework was fun today."

I liked how Tyler enjoyed his time with Ian, but I didn't want him to get attached, either. Ian had come because I was sick, and he wouldn't have needed to if Kate had been here.

It's just this one time. It'll be fine. You're thinking too much.

I stroked Tyler's cheek, looking at him adoringly.

"Here you go, Abby." Ian placed the bowl and a spoon in front of me. "Be careful. It's hot."

Steam rose from the chicken soup, and my stomach rumbled in expectation. Slices of carrot, celery, onion, and diced chicken bobbed in the hot liquid when I blew over the surface.

"Ian. I don't know what to say. You cleaned up my mess, and you helped Tyler with his homework. Thank you for everything." I offered him a grateful smile. "Can you come over every day?" I laughed.

Ian snorted, standing beside Tyler, and ruffled his hair. "Don't worry about it. Besides, I had a helper."

I gawked when Tyler shrugged and didn't push Ian away. He didn't like people touching his hair.

"Aren't you going to eat?" I picked up the spoon.

Ian strolled to the kitchen and came back with two white bowls of ice cream. "Tyler and I ate soup and sandwiches, and now we're having dessert. I remembered we both love chocolate chip ice cream. I bought some when I bought dinner. I hope you don't mind."

"No, of course not. Let me pay for—"

Ian shook his head and settled back in a seat across from me. "No paying for anything. You can make it up to me with a homecooked meal. I have heard from my sources that you are an excellent chef. How does that sound?"

"Yes!" Tyler punched the air and shrank when he realized he was being loud. He lowered his gaze and clanked his spoon on the bowl.

Ian and I laughed.

While I ate, Tyler and Ian talked about different video games in between pale, rounded spoons of ice cream. Tyler's eyes lit up when he laughed. He looked so happy, and I tried not to stare at Ian. His deep chuckle made me smile.

We sat around the table as if we were a family. A mom, dad, and son. This was what it would have been like if Steve were alive. Tyler having a father as a role model. Family dinners. It felt strange to have another man in our house.

"Do your parents live in Kauai, too?" My spoon clinked on the bowl.

"No, but they visit. We grew up in New York. I see them two or three times a year."

Tyler wiped his mouth with the back of his hand. I cringed and handed him a napkin.

Ian swallowed ice cream. "My older sister, Iliana, is a pediatrician. She's married with twin girls. They're two years old."

"Awww." I smiled.

"My younger brother Isaac was a dentist, but he got into real estate at the same time I did, thanks to Lee. He lives in Florida, but he visits."

"That's wonderful. Congrats to Isaac. He's brave for switching his career."

He gave me a curt nod with a tight-lipped smile. "So ..." His gaze traveled from the bookshelf to the hearth. There was a photo on the mantel of Steve, me, and Tyler when he'd been two. "That's your ...?"

"That's Steve."

"He has a kind face. I'm sure he was a great husband and father." Ian smiled at my son.

The Seashell of 'Ohana

I spooned up soup and let it fall, putting off a response. Opening up to Ian was easy, but this seemed too intimate. I needed to relax. Ian was asking questions to be polite, but small talk about my dead husband was strange.

I had put away a large portrait of the three of us that had hung over the fireplace because it hurt too much. But I kept the smaller photo on the mantel. I didn't want Tyler to forget what his father looked like. Steve had passed away when Tyler was three, and he didn't have many memories of him.

Silence pressed as Ian continued to eat his ice cream, and I doggedly ate my soup.

"Have you been all over the world like Lee?" I asked.

Ian's eyes rounded as if he were surprised by the question. "I flew back and forth from New York to Los Angeles, mostly. After I retired as a stockbroker and partnered up with Lee, I traveled to China, South Korea, the Philippines, Singapore, and more places I can't remember right now. So, to answer your question, yes. That was a very long answer." He snorted. "How about you?"

I swirled my spoon inside the mostly empty bowl and peered up at him. "I was born in Los Angeles and lived there until Steve, Ty, and I moved to New York. After Steve passed away, Ty and I moved to Kauai, and we've been here ever since."

Ian set down his spoon. "Why did you move to New York when your family lived in Los Angeles?"

I wrung a strand of hair around my ear. Sometimes I wondered if we should have stayed in LA. Perhaps he wouldn't have taken the job if I'd told him I wanted to stay close to my family. Then he wouldn't have worked so hard, and it wouldn't have changed Steve's health. Even years later, I fell into the useless trap of imagining how we could have prevented the cancer that had taken his life.

I shifted on the cushion and crossed my legs. "I got an offer to work at one of New York's finest galleries, and Steve got a high-paying offer at a dream job. It couldn't have been more perfect timing for the both of us. So we went for it."

Ian glanced at Tyler, who was licking the spoon, then at me. "So after you moved to Kauai, you haven't left the island?"

"I've been too busy," I said.

"My parents didn't travel much until Lee's parents practically dragged them out of the house. If it weren't for Lee's parents, mine would be hermits. I'm kind of that way. I mostly travel for work.

Sometimes you need that one person to give you a little push. Would you like to travel one day?"

My gaze went to Tyler, who was nodding. I let out a soft chuckle. "Yes. And Tyler would love to, too."

Ian spread his lips into a wide grin. "Good. Then we should make it happen."

I didn't know how to interpret *we*, so I let it go. After Ian went home, I tucked Tyler in bed. I went to my room to wash up but got distracted by my cell flashing. I had several missed calls and tons of texts.

> Kate: Just checking up on you.

> Kate: How are you doing?

> Kate: Hello?

> Kate: Is Ian still there?

I shouldn't be mad at her, but I couldn't help thinking that maybe she'd set this all up. I read her last text.

> Kate: Do I need to come over?

I thumbed a reply and sent it.

> Abby: Sorry. I had my phone off. Ian just
> left. I' ll tell you about it tomorrow.

Chapter Thirteen — The Interview

The next morning, I arrived at the gallery refreshed and ready to conquer the day. I felt fortunate and proud of how the business had thrived. But being sick yesterday had put me a day behind, and I still wanted to go back to bed. The thoughts of deadlines and unfinished paintings had me nearly hyperventilating.

It's going to be fine. One project at a time.

I scrolled down a list of clients' names on the computer in the back room. Mr. Thomas's name had been crossed off. Kate's project. She had finished it on time.

Mrs. Worthington, my client, had requested two oil paintings. She wanted me to paint Rainbow Falls and Akaka Falls, both located in Hilo, the big island. I had completed *Rainbow Falls* the other day. The vibrant colors of the rainbow arched over the splashing waterfall, sparkling and lifelike. It might turn out to be one of my favorites.

When I scanned down the remaining names, I felt an anxiety attack coming on again. Too many. It was fantastic for our business, but at the same time, we needed help.

Through text, Kate had let me know that she would be coming in around lunchtime and that she had interviewed a couple of artists while I'd been sick. I would have one interviewee this morning.

I sat in front of my easel next to the supply shelf and examined the unfinished canvas staring back at me. The ocean was done, but I needed to add some turtles on the sand. I turned to my finished paintings, which were hung by the desk to motivate me, but I kept thinking of Ian.

My cell phone on the table beside me vibrated in the quiet, startling me. I was pleasantly surprised by Ian's text.

Ian: I hope you're feeling better.

Abby: Thanks to your miracle chicken soup,
I'm at work.

Ian: I'd like to think it was my presence and

not the soup.

I added a laughing emoji and was surprised how easily the conversation flowed, like two good friends. No response came, so I figured we were done.

"Abby. Liam, your eleven o'clock is here," Stella announced through the speakerphone.

I had forgotten to look over his résumé, and I had no questions prepared. It was unlike me to be last-minute, reacting to things as they happened instead of planning. No matter. I would wing it. I blamed it on Ian.

I took off the apron, tossed it over the stool, and strode out the door. Stella had her elbow pressed on her desk, her chin on her raised fist. Her eyes were fixed on a young, handsome man, who was running a finger along the wing of an angel statue on the shelf by the window.

He wore dark slacks and a long-sleeve button-up white dress shirt and carried a black leather case. The sunlight bounced off his sandy brown hair, and his skin glowed like he had just come back from the beach.

The patter of my flats on the tile broke his stare, and he turned to me with a warm grin, brightening up the room. Or, maybe I should say, he brightened up Stella. Her smile reached her eyes.

Liam met me by the sofa then gave me a sturdy handshake. "Hello, Abby. It's nice to meet you. I've heard such great things about you and your sister, Kate."

He knew my sister's name. A point for him. He'd done his homework. And he had the cutest dimples.

"Thank you," I said. "I hope you won't be disappointed after the interview. Would you like something to drink?"

He flashed a glance over to Stella. "Your lovely assistant already asked, but I'm fine."

Stella tried to hide her coloring cheeks by looking at the computer screen. I gestured to a small glass table and two simple metal chairs at the far back corner, away from the window and potential customers.

I didn't want to take him to the backroom, where it was crowded and messy. Besides, I wanted Stella's opinion. She also had to like the person we hired. Kate had arranged the furniture for her interviews yesterday, and the back corner was the perfect spot.

"So, tell me about yourself." I eased into the hard chair in front of Liam and crossed my legs.

Liam pulled a leather-bound portfolio from the case by his feet and handed it to me. I ran a palm over the smooth leather and spread the portfolio open on the glass table.

"I've lived in Kauai all my life," Liam said. "I graduated with a degree in fine arts." He pointed to the résumé he'd placed in front of me. "That has more detail about my classes and awards I won in college. I don't have much experience besides teaching online, but my portfolio will give you a sense of my style and vision. I also have a website, which is listed on the bottom of my résumé."

I used to be furious when the person who interviewed me asked questions I had clearly answered in my cover letter and on my résumé. Giving him the same treatment made me feel unprofessional. I turned the page, admiring the sketches of people, animals, and buildings.

Liam sounded confident, and I liked his honesty, and his portfolio was diverse, unique, and impressive.

"I've also taken classes in photography," he added as I continued to flip through his work. "If you get a chance to look at my website, you'll see recent work."

Photography was not listed as a requirement in our ad, but it sure would be a bonus.

I handed Liam back his portfolio. "We don't pay hourly. The position pays based on commission. You wouldn't have to actively look for your clients, but you might have to work to a client's specifications. Are you okay with that?"

He leaned to the side to drop his portfolio inside his case. "I'm fine with commission. Creating art takes hours of work, and sometimes, almost as much time thinking. It's practically impossible to charge fairly for all the time spent on a piece."

If I could, I would hire him on the spot.

"Well, Liam." I clasped my hands together on my lap. "I like what I see. Kate and I will be discussing the candidates at the end of this week after we finish up the interviews. Then we'll let you know."

"Sounds great." He extended his hand, warm and firm, across the table. His dimples deepened when he grinned. "Thank you for your time. And if I'm hired, without trying to sound arrogant, you won't regret it."

I rose and walked with him toward the door.

Stella rolled her swivel chair around to face him. She pretended to be busy, but I knew she had been eavesdropping. She offered him her best sunshine smile.

As I reached to open the door for Liam, Kate entered. Wind chimes tinkled. Liam called Kate's name to catch her attention, introduced himself, and left. Another point to him for recognizing her.

"Liam has cute dimples." Kate strolled toward the sofa.

"*Right?*" Stella's fingers danced away on the keyboard.

Kate wore no makeup and had her hair tied back into a ponytail. Her attire of jeans and an old T-shirt meant all business.

"He's organized." I walked toward my sister. "He was prepared for the interview. He even knew your name and recognized you. Impressive."

"Isn't he?" Stella's gray eyes turned dreamy. "I think you should hire him."

I leaned on the back of the sofa and anchored my hands on the cool leather. "You're clearly biased. You don't get to say anything in this. You want me to hire him based on looks."

"So not fair." She rolled her eyes and let out a playful scoff. "I do everything around here."

It was partly true. While Stella took care of the business end, Kate and I painted all day.

Stella added, "At least allow me to have some eye candy for all the work I put in. I might even stay overtime for free if *he's* around."

Kate glanced between Stella and me and walked to the refreshment table. "Setting aside his cute face, how was the interview?" She picked up a bottle of water and twisted open the cap.

"He doesn't have much experience, but I think he would fit right in," I said. "He's pretty comfortable in a variety of styles and media, and he does photography."

"Photography? Perfect." Kate took a drink and strolled toward the back room. "The others I interviewed wanted to be paid by the hour."

I followed behind her and said, "We can't hire him just yet. We have other interviews."

Kate held open the door and entered behind me. While she went to her workstation, I checked my phone. Ian had left a message.

**Ian: Wanted to let you know I'm stopping
by in the afternoon.**

I placed my phone down and turned. Kate stood in front of me, her eyebrows arching.

"Yes?" I narrowed my eyes at her and tied the apron. "Did you get paint on me somehow? You know you're good at that."

Kate scowled, looking offended, then turned her lips downward like a pouting child. She slapped my shoulder lightly. "Anyway, who were you texting?"

"Wasn't texting, and it's none of your business."

She glared as she walked backward to her stool. "If you don't want to tell me who your secret admirer is, fine with me." She sat and picked up a brush from the rolling tray. "But I know who he is," she sang.

Although my sister and I were edging closer to thirty, we would probably never stop acting like the two kids we'd always been together. That included the good and the bad, and sometimes we bickered like teenagers. Though I loved working with her and seeing her every day, sometimes we needed space, especially when she got into my business.

I sat on the stool next to her and squeezed the yellow oil tube on the palette. "He? How do you know? Could easily be a *she*."

Kate shrugged sheepishly and flicked her fan brush over the white clouds to blend the paint into the blue sky. "Because of the way you smiled."

"It was just Ian." I cleared my throat as heat rose up my neck. Ian would be here later, and Kate would find out he had messaged me.

Kate leaned sideways and bumped her shoulder to mine. "See, that wasn't so hard. Love you, sis." She gave me a quick peck on the cheek. "I'll go pick up the kids after school. You stay here."

Love you, too. Thank you for being my rock.

Chapter Fourteen — After School

K ate picked up Bridget and Tyler after school and brought them to the gallery. The kids settled in the back room while I discussed the inventory with Kate and Stella at her desk.

Wind chimes tinkled, and the door opened. Ian and his friend strolled in just as we finished. My cheeks heated, and I offered a small smile when Ian and I locked gazes.

Ian's friend had dark hair and brown eyes. The thickness of both of their eyebrows and strong jawline were the same. They looked similar.

"This is Isaac," Ian said, his eyes wide with amusement.

"I see why you wanted me to check out this gallery." Isaac took our hands one by one and kissed the backs of them. "It's so nice to meet you, pretty ladies."

"Isaac? Isaac, your brother?" I said, my voice louder than I had intended.

Ian shrugged. "He popped in unexpectedly. Sometimes he does that."

"I've heard so much about you, Abby." His devilish smirk was the same as Ian's.

When Ian had told me about Isaac, his brother the dentist, I had imagined him reserved. But he was just as confident, playful, and outgoing. And as good-looking.

"Oh," I said nervously.

"Don't worry. It's all good," Isaac said. He glanced about the room. "Ian has good taste in … art." His gaze landed on me.

I was pretty sure he wasn't talking about art.

Ian cleared his throat and lightly shoved his brother. "What Isaac is trying to say is that he would love to see some of your paintings." Ian narrowed his eyes at his brother. "Don't waste Abby's time."

Footsteps pattered across the tile floor from the back room.

Bridget and Tyler came rushing out to greet Ian and his brother. While the rest chatted and laughed by Stella's desk, I guided Isaac to the paintings on the wall.

Isaac looked from left to right as I explained who had painted what and their inspiration. He took his time examining each painting as if he were an expert. When I glanced over my shoulder, I caught Ian watching me. He smiled and turned back to the conversation with Stella.

Isaac purchased a total of five paintings for his properties and a sculpture of a unicorn and an angel with her wings slightly open. While he continued to admire a painting of the palm trees on the beach, I finished the transaction and returned to him.

"Do you have any questions, Isaac?" I said.

"No, but those are going to look great on the plain white walls." He leaned closer. "By the way, thanks for being a bright light in Ian's life. When our mother passed away, Ian took it the hardest."

Ian hadn't told me his mother had passed away. When?

It wasn't my business, but Ian and I were getting to know each other. Maybe he didn't feel comfortable telling me. It must've been recent. Was that the reason Ian had asked me about Steve? Maybe I was reading into this too much. If he'd wanted me to know, he would have mentioned it. But I could ask his brother since he'd brought it up.

"When did—"

Ian slid himself between us. "Seems like you two are finished. Isaac isn't pestering you, is he?" He glanced at his brother, then me.

"Pestering?" Isaac hiked an eyebrow. "Be careful what you say, big brother. I'll tell Abby something embarrassing about you."

Ian edged closer to me like he wanted to get away from Isaac. "You see what I have to deal with, Abby? At least you have a nice sister."

I crossed my arms and shook my head at Kate. "I don't know, Ian. Sometimes she's a handful, too."

I wanted to know more about his mother and what had happened to her. I wanted to hug him and let him know I knew his pain. People grieve in their own way. Losing a loved one can often bind those left behind. And because of this, I wanted to be a better friend to Ian.

Thanks for being a bright light in Ian's life, Isaac had said. Sometimes just being there for someone made a difference, but I didn't know what I had said or done to help.

"Handful?" Kate chimed in. She leaned back on Stella's desk and frowned. Tyler and Bridget giggled from either side of her.

Stella rose from her chair. "How do you think I feel? I have to deal with both of them every day." She cast a glance between Kate and me with a smile. "But I love them, so I put up with them. And they pay me, so I have to say that."

Everyone laughed, even Bridget and Tyler.

A clap from Isaac caught all of our attention. "I'm getting hungry. I'm taking everyone to dinner."

I didn't want to disappoint Ian, but I had so much to do. I straightened the tea bags in the box to delay what I was about to say.

"I hate to be the party pooper, but you all go on ahead and enjoy yourselves," I said.

"Party pooper?" Tyler let out a laugh, and he and Bridget dissolved into a fit of giggles.

"What?" Isaac frowned, walking toward his brother. "Not an option. We all go, or we all stay."

"Thanks for wanting to include me," I said, "but unless you want customers pounding on my door, I've got to get work done."

Ian leveled his gaze with mine. "Isaac and I will order dinner, and we'll all eat here. If it's okay with everyone, we'll grab Chinese. I know the perfect place."

While the Bordonaro brothers took the kids with them to pick up food, Kate and I dove into our work. When they came back, Ian spread the containers of chow mien, kung pao chicken, and assorted vegetables on the table. Isaac handed everyone a paper plate and utensils, and I passed out water bottles.

Stella and I sat at the corner table where I had held the interview. Kate sat with Bridget, and Tyler squeezed in between Ian and Isaac on the other sofa.

We talked about movies, schools, and places Isaac had traveled. Sometimes my eyes met Ian's, and I'd smile and turn away. Other times, I stole glances at him and wondered what he was thinking.

Was he thinking of his mother while putting on a fake smile? After Steve had passed away, I'd pretended that all was fine. For years, I made sure people didn't regard me as broken, grieving too much. Nobody could see my heart splitting or the amount of energy it took just to breathe.

"The Bordonaro brothers are such gentlemen," Stella whispered from across the glass table. "So not fair. Why do you and Kate know all the cute men?"

I let out a quick laugh and twirled wooden chopsticks around the chow mien noodles. "Do you want me to find out if Isaac or Ian is single?"

"Nah," she said between chewing. "We don't know how long Isaac is staying. And Ian is yours."

"What?" I coughed, my throat burning from a stray red pepper in the kung pao chicken. I sucked down half a bottle of water. "Ian isn't mine. We're not together. What gave you that idea?"

Stella rolled her eyes up to the white flat ceiling and let out an exaggerated sigh. "Seriously, not again. First your sister and now you."

Stella had predicted Lee and Kate would get together long before either of them had known.

"Never mind," she said. "Besides, I have my eyes on my sandy-brown-haired Liam with dimples."

I shook my head and took a bite of broccoli. If we hired him, I would discourage interoffice dating. Working together might be a problem if things went wrong. I didn't want to sound like a nagging boss, so I left the topic alone. I, too, had to remain professional.

Stella twirled noodles around her fork and tilted her head toward the sofa. "Looks like someone is attached to Ian."

I glanced over at Tyler. Ian pointed at a broccoli, and Tyler ate it.

My Tyler had *eaten* broccoli?

Ian placed an arm around my son and patted his back. Tyler gave him a big smile. The interaction tugged hard at my heartstrings. Tyler wouldn't tell me directly, but I knew he missed having a father figure.

Isaac placed his plate down and said, "So, you're all invited to Ian's beach house this Saturday."

What? Stella had distracted me, and I had missed the conversation.

"And Isaac will be cooking." Ian tossed a crumpled napkin at his brother. "That's what you get for opening my house without asking me first." He turned to Kate and the kids, then cast a quick look my way. "I was planning to invite you all anyway. And I have lots of chocolate chip ice cream."

"Yeah!" the kids said at the same time.

"Can we go?" Tyler pinned his gaze on me, begging me with those puppy eyes I couldn't resist.

"Sure. Why not?" I was already behind anyway. What was one more day?

More cheers erupted from the kids and from the Bordonaro brothers.

Chapter Fifteen — Alone With My Thoughts

Work went by faster than a wink, that week. On Saturday, I woke up at seven in the morning despite having nothing pressing to do. When I wasn't rushing to get Tyler off to school or having to go to work, being alone in the early morning felt peaceful.

Instead of lounging in bed, I decided to go jogging. Tyler would still be asleep when I got back home, but just in case, I wrote a note and left it on his bed next to him. He couldn't miss the plain white paper.

> Ty,
> I went jogging. I'll be back soon.
> I love you across the galaxies and beyond.

Working long hours had me neglecting my fitness, and I really needed the run this morning. Exercising not only helped me reduce stress, it was my time to be alone with my thoughts and sometimes forget the world.

After stretching, I shoved my phone in the back of my black workout pants and locked the door behind me. I inhaled a deep, cool breath and peered up to the fluffy clouds. When Tyler had been five, one of his favorite games had been picking fanciful shapes out of the clouds. He'd stopped playing that game with me, but the clouds overhead this morning looked like angel wings, like the seashell I'd found on the beach.

My feet pounded on the sidewalk as I ran past the houses, palm trees, and tall grasses. I waved at a man with a large dog as he came toward me. When I jogged out to the main street, cars zoomed by, mostly headed toward public beaches.

Sweat beaded my forehead, and my lungs pumped. This kind of adrenaline felt so good. On my way home, I stopped by Izzy's Café, my favorite after-run reward.

Izzy would be happy to see me. At eight in the morning, I was often her first customer. However, the woman behind the counter wasn't Izzy. She looked to be in her late twenties.

"Good morning," she said.

My pulse kicked up, and my mind ran wild. Was Izzy in the hospital? Heart attack? Stroke? When people weren't where they were supposed to be, morbid thoughts always came first.

Slow down. It could be nothing.

"Is Izzy working today?" I asked.

"Izzy took the day off. I'm her daughter."

I let out a breath of relief. I could see the resemblance in the shape of her eyes and cute nose.

She smiled. "What can I get you?"

I wanted to ask her if Izzy was doing okay. Izzy had never taken a day off, but I didn't know if she would share. After all, she had no idea who I was. I glanced at the menu that hung on the back wall, written in white chalk, not sure why I bothered to look. I always ordered the same thing.

"Hot hazelnut latte with soy milk, please."

Izzy's daughter wasn't a talker like her mom. It hadn't been long since I'd last seen Izzy, but her absence made me sad. I missed her.

When she passed me the paper cup, I spotted an angel-wing tattoo on her wrist. Two wings, connected at the top tip, fanning outward. Like the seashell I had at home.

Some people just loved tattoos, and many people got them for sentimental reasons. I wondered what her story was or if she even had one. Maybe she got the tattoo after someone she loved passed away. Though I was itching to ask, I decided to let it go.

Tyler was still asleep when I returned home. I leaned against the doorframe and watched my son as I sipped my warm latte. His chest rose and fell in a steady rhythm, reminding me of the days when he'd been an infant, sleeping in his crib. Steve and I had watched Tyler for hours.

A photo of Steve that I kept on Tyler's bedside table was facedown. I wondered if Tyler had been looking at his father last night while in bed.

"Mom?" Tyler fluttered his eyelids. "What are you doing? Is it time to go to school?"

I smiled. "No, Ty. It's Saturday."

He sat up, his eyes growing wide with excitement. "Shiver me timbers. We're going to Ian's house today." He got up faster than he would on a school day and opened his closet door. "Can I have pancakes for breakfast?"

"Only if you help me make them."

"Aye. Cool." He gave me a thumbs up and flashed all his teeth.

He looked so much like Steve, at that moment. He rushed out of his room, and his infectious joy for life pulled me along with him.

Chapter Sixteen — Ian's House

I followed the GPS and turned on the next street. In Poipu, most houses were separated by a good-sized lot, for privacy, but the space was even more prevalent in this neighborhood. When we turned onto Ian's street, sunlight spilled like molten gold across the ocean, flecks of light waving hypnotically. The low drifting clouds gave an illusion that you could walk straight into heaven. Simply breathtaking.

Ian's house was one story, but had a lot of windows and sleek, modern lines. Not as grand as Lee's, but gorgeous and right on the beach. White, pink, and red plumerias lined the cobblestone walkway up to the grand double front door. The flowers were the crowning touch on a lovely house, creating a warm and inviting approach saturated with a delicate scent.

I hiked up the bag strap over my shoulder with all of Tyler's things and rang the doorbell.

Isaac squinted in the slanting sunlight. He greeted me with open arms and high-fived Tyler. "Ahoy, me hearties. Welcome to my brother's humble home. Everyone is in the back. I'll show you the way."

He must play *Buccaneers versus Skeletons*, too.

Tyler ran past me in the foyer. In the center was a brass table with a large vase of assorted lilies and bird of paradise blooms. I followed Isaac past a family room with a huge flat-screen television and U-shaped brown sofas.

I looked for photos of Ian's family, but there were none. Perhaps he didn't bother with such décor, since this wasn't his permanent home.

He did hang paintings, though. *Wailua Falls*, the one Isaac had bought from my gallery, and a large photo of the Poipu beach that Kate had taken hung near the TV. I'd thought Isaac had bought them for his properties, but I was humbled that Ian had them displayed in his home.

On the opposite wall near the kitchen was a painting Kate called *Mr. Medici*. Ian had bought that about three years ago. The canvas measured eighty by eighty inches, and it was a muddy blob of mismatched colors. It looked like someone had vomited paint onto the canvas. But art was art.

That piece of art had a long story, well known among their friends. The short version: Kate messed around with paint in the backroom and accidentally got some on Lee's button-up dress shirt.

Isaac noticed me staring at another art piece in the family room, so he stopped short. "Oh, Ian wanted that, so I let him have it. But that means I'm short one *Wailua Falls*. I'll have to either stop by your gallery, or I'll go through your website."

"You can stop by any time," I said.

I strolled near the long hallway that led to the bedrooms. I wondered what they looked like. My eyes wandered to the crown molding from corner to corner throughout the house. I'd always wanted crown molding, but my ceiling wasn't high enough.

We went through a kitchen with white cabinets and upscale stainless-steel appliances, spotless and not in use. Perhaps we were cooking out—or someone had cheated and ordered food. When we stepped outside through the sliding glass door, I put on my sunglasses.

Breathtaking.

I passed by the built-in BBQ. In the center was the swimming pool, not as big as Lee's, but a good size. There was no need for a pool, though. The backyard extended to the beach, and coconut trees surrounded the area—pure paradise by anyone's standards.

Warm, grainy sand pressed between my toes and inside my flip-flops as I made footprints toward the others. The light breeze tousled my hair, and the sun bathed my skin at the perfect spring temperature.

Kate and Stella were seated at a wooden table with drinks in their hands. Two large beach umbrellas cast shade over them. Bridget was sitting on the edge of the pool, kicking water and reading a book. When she spotted Tyler, she tossed her book into her backpack and jogged toward us with a warm smile.

Bridget's blonde hair seemed lighter under the sun, and her blue eyes almost gray. Kate and Stella heard Bridget calling Tyler's name and got up to greet us. Tyler and Bridget rushed off to *play Buccaneers versus Skeletons* on her tablet at the table by the pool.

"Abby, you look so cute." Stella kissed my cheek. "Wearing shorts and a tank makes you look younger, playful, and flirty, boss." She lightly shoved me.

Peering over my sunglasses, I pierced my gaze to hers. I couldn't see her eyes through the dark-shaded glasses, but she stopped talking.

I placed my bag down on the sand, sat beside Kate, and watched

Lee and Ian walk toward us from the ocean. Nobody could tell I was looking, because of my sunglasses, but heat blazed up my neck and down my middle, and it wasn't from the warm sun.

Actually, I might have gawked. So did my sister and Stella. It was like watching two hot models in a swimsuit commercial shoot with water dripping from their hair, down their six-packs, and lower. The sun caught the sheen of sunscreen at that precise moment, giving the illusion that their bodies had been sleeked with oil.

Not going to lie. I couldn't take my eyes off Ian.

"Holy hotness," Stella muttered under her breath. "Sorry for staring, but damn. I've never seen two sexy Italian men in one place before."

Kate lowered her sunglasses, narrowing her eyes at Stella, then raised her glasses again. "I don't blame you. You can look all you want, but Lee is mine."

Ian's lips tugged higher. As he strutted toward me, his eyes never left mine. I rose to greet them. Lee gave me a peck on the cheek, then got a towel and a shirt from Kate.

"Hello, Abby," Ian said in a flirty tone.

Ian grabbed his towel off the lounge chair. After he dried himself, he put on a muscle shirt, then enclosed me in a hug and handed me the glass of piña colada he had grabbed from the built-in bar behind us.

"If it tastes horrible, you can blame Lee." Ian snorted. "If it tastes perfect, well, you can thank me however you like."

I smiled and sat back down next to Kate and took a sip. "Does Isaac need help with dinner?"

Ian pulled a chair next to mine. "Don't worry about it. We're catering, and Isaac went back in to take care of last-minute business."

When Bridget and Tyler got in the water up to their knees, I sat up straighter and watched them like a hawk. This time, there would be no mistake. No practice holding breath.

"We're still on for the auction, right?" Ian asked.

"You can count on us being there." Lee handed Ian a beer, and they clanked bottles.

Stella pulled her mouth away from the bottle. "You're going to the auction at the Romanos' mansion? The one they have every year?"

"Yes," Ian said.

Ian had said 'the Romanos' place.' He hadn't mentioned we were going to a mansion.

Stella released a soft whistle. "I heard they expect you to buy something. Is that right?"

Ian's broad shoulders touched the back of his chair. "Technically, you're not buying, you're auctioning, so if someone outbids you, then you have no choice."

"Yeah, but it would suck if you really wanted one of the paintings from our gallery, and you were outbid." She snorted.

Ian, who was just about to take another sip of his drink, stopped midway. "True."

"What's the cause that it benefits?" Kate asked.

Ian didn't answer right away. His eyes were set on the horizon, the periwinkle sky darkening as the sun dipped lower. After he took a drink, he said, "Dementia."

Something about the slow, intense way he'd said it seemed so personal. I would ask him later if we got the chance to be alone. I looked over at Lee to see if I could read the answer in his expression, but his gaze was fixed on Bridget and Tyler.

"Anyway, Stella," Ian continued, his eyes going from absent to gleaming. "If you're free, you should come with us."

She shifted uncomfortably, leaning her elbow on the armrest. "I would love to go, but I don't have a ticket. I heard they were expensive. Abby and Kate don't pay me enough to afford a ticket to that shindig."

"What?" I squealed, even though I knew she was teasing.

Stella stuck out her palm as if to stop me from attacking her. "Just kidding, Abby. You and Kate are generous with my pay."

"We want to keep you happy," Kate said. "You know too much. Now we have to keep you."

"I can get an extra ticket for you, Stella." Ian paused and glanced over to the house. "Actually, Isaac has an extra one. He could take you. I don't think he asked anyone yet."

As if on cue, Isaac shouted from the house. "Dinner is ready!"

Chapter Seventeen — Under the Moonlight

Isaac looked adorable with a black apron around his waist. He had arranged the dishes, utensils, and wine glasses on the eight-seater dining table. Flower petals scattered around lit candles, providing an elegant ambiance.

"So pretty." Bridget's blue eyes twinkled brighter under the glass light fixture.

"Nice job, Isaac," Stella said.

We took turns complimenting him as we sat down to eat. Chicken with pineapple, seafood linguini, rice pilaf with sliced almonds, and assorted salad, catered from the finest restaurant. Every single dish was nothing short of amazing.

Ian raised his glass, and though he was talking to everyone, he looked at me. "I would like to make a toast. To old and new friends. May your house be warm and your cups be full."

Glasses clinked as we exchanged smiles.

"You know," Stella said after taking a sip, "you can invite me anytime. You all eat so well."

"Well ..." Isaac leaned closer to Stella, who was sitting next to him. "I need a date—"

"Saturday?" Stella said before he could finish.

Isaac furrowed his brow. "It's for the—"

"The auction. And I would love to go with you."

Isaac cackled, his eyes gleaming against the candlelight. "That was easy. I like her. Now I have a date."

We laughed and talked and enjoyed our meal. As utensils clanked and glasses thudded on the table, I wondered how long it had been since Ian and Isaac's mother had passed away.

After we had the dessert Kate and Lee had brought—cream puffs with vanilla ice cream in the middle—we sat in the family room. While everyone played video games with the kids, I snuck out to the beach.

I sat on the cool sand and extended my legs just to the point where the water met my toes. I shivered, staring at the full, silver moon and the countless stars. The scenic view reminded me of a time when Steve and I had gone to the beach with our friends after finals. We'd splashed in the water and yelled like children, relieved to be done with the semester.

The cold ocean water lapped over my feet, breaking my reverie. I shuddered as I released air from my heavy heart. I should go back inside before anyone realized I was gone, but I loved being out here in the dark with my thoughts. The solitude was serene among the waves and stars, and I didn't want to go in just yet.

A warm, soft weight draped around my shoulders, and I jerked, my heart thundering. The roar of the crashing waves had prevented me from hearing anyone sneaking up on me. I hadn't thought anyone would notice that I was missing, at least for a bit longer.

Ian plopped down next to me. He was wearing a T-shirt and his swim trunks.

"Thank you for the blanket." I patted the fabric over my shoulders. "You didn't have to come find me."

"And let you have all the fun?" He grinned and dipped his feet in the foam when the water rolled in. "It's a beautiful night, isn't it?"

I leaned back, arms behind me, my hands anchored in the sand. "You're lucky you get this view every night."

"But no one to share it with," he said in a somber tone.

I gave him a sidelong glance. The moonlight cascaded over half of his features, leaving stark shadows. He looked content, but his eyes told another story—of longing, perhaps, or sadness.

"And not every night," he added. "Only when I'm here."

"Where is your permanent home?"

Ian shuffled his feet in the wet sand, making footprints. "It depends on work and depends on how much Lee misses me." He snickered.

"And your brother?"

He gazed up at the moon, then back to me with a soft, defeated sigh. "I didn't tell you earlier because I don't like talking about my mother. I'm full of guilt, and it's hard to let it go."

I crossed my legs and tightened the blanket as a chill breeze swirled. "You don't have to tell me anything, Ian. But I promise I won't judge you. I'm here to listen. Sometimes you just have to let it out."

Ian nodded and brought his knees up to his chest. "My mother passed away less than a year ago. She died at the hospital from complications of a stroke, but she also had a long, painful battle with dementia. The auction will support a local dementia charity. I'm on the board."

"I'm so sorry," I said. "But it's great what you're doing."

He gave me a tight-lipped smile and continued looking over the ocean. "Everyone should contribute what they can to the causes that are important to them. We all need to do our part. I have a lot of guilt for not spending time with my mother. I always put my work above her. I thought …" His voice cracked, and he paused to find his words. "I'd thought we had time."

The breeze had picked up. I threw half of my blanket around him. His arms went up like he would protest, but instead, he snuggled closer.

I let the silence between us sink in for a bit as we stared at the night sky. I needed to think through my thoughts without saying something meaningless.

"That's the thing about time. There's *never* enough." The words came easy because I had lived them. I understood.

"That's true," he said, resigned. "I think I was in denial, which made me drown myself in work even more. Her dementia got so bad that she …" He glanced down at his sand-covered toes. "She didn't know who I was. That was the worst. Isaac quit his job when our mother passed away and decided to partner with me. I'm glad he did so I could spend time with him. I hardly got to see him before."

"And your sister?"

"The three of us see each other as often as we can. She took some time off to help our father. She's with him now. I was with him before Iliana took over." Ian shuffled sand with his feet. "When my mother had dementia, we watched her wither and deteriorate little by little. That was the hardest part. But even when you prepare for death, it's still difficult."

I knew that feeling well. There had been times when I could barely get out of bed, let alone do something simple like eat, but somehow, I found the strength to take care of Tyler. Thankfully, my parents and Kate had been there for me during the worst days.

"My dad is doing better," Ian added. "But it took a while. I don't think anyone can understand unless they've experienced losing a loved one. It's heart-wrenching, and there are no words to describe the pain."

"I understand." I released a long sigh.

As if he'd realized something, his eyes grew wide. He turned to me and grabbed my hand.

"Abby, I'm so sorry. Of course, you know. Here I am rambling on about my mother, and I was insensitive about Steve."

"Ian, please. It's okay. Steve passed away years ago, but your wound is fresh. You need to talk about it."

Ian kissed the hand he held and let go. "I appreciate you listening to me. You're so easy to talk to."

I stiffened, surprised. But I should be used to his casual displays of affection by now. First, the kiss at the market and every time he greeted me.

"You can talk to me anytime," I said. "I think it's my best quality, next to painting, of course." I needed to say something to make light of things.

"I'm sure you have other talents. I'm going to find out. Now that you're my therapist, whether you like it or not, we'll have to see more of each other." He bumped his shoulder into mine, his fun, carefree side replacing the serious one.

See more of each other. "What was your mother like?" I asked to stop blushing.

Ian grabbed a handful of wet sand and began to make a pile. "My mother was amazing. When my grandparents emigrated from Italy to the States, they struggled to make ends meet. My mother worked at her parents' bakery while earning a college degree. She paid her tuition and she was so proud of that. My parents were upper-middle class, but you could never tell. They didn't flash their material wealth. My mom didn't own hundreds of purses or have a closet full of designer clothes, but she could have."

"I didn't know her, but just from what you're telling me, I respect her."

He scooped more wet sand and let it stream between his fingers. "My mother used to say that our gift to her would be giving her grandchildren. At least she got to see my sister's kids."

"And one day, she'll see yours, and your brother's, from above." The wind picked up and plucked at my hair. I tried holding it down, but the strands flew about wildly, whipping my face and getting caught in my mouth. I tossed the blanket over our heads. "There, it's much quieter."

"Our little secret place." His lips curled wickedly as he locked his gaze with mine.

The beautiful night sky disappeared, and the sound of water lapping over the shore faded. No one was here except for Ian and me.

Ian broke whatever was happening between us and said, "I never heard my parents fight about anything. There was a lot of love and respect for each other. They were like two halves of a soul. If there is such thing as soulmates, then she was his, and he was hers. I would like to find my other soul one day. I know there is someone out there that is a perfect match for me."

My heart thudded out of my chest. *If there ever was such a thing as soulmates, then he was mine, and I was his.* I had thought that about Steve when we'd first met. But why did it give me goose bumps?

Ian lowered the blanket to our shoulders and wiped wet sand from something he held. "I'm so happy Lee found Kate. They deserve each other. And Kate is so good with Bridget."

"My sister is good with kids. Kate got a lot of practice with Tyler. She was over every weekend to help me, at first, but things changed when we moved to New York."

I wanted to talk about how wonderful life had been in New York until Steve had gotten sick. Then everything went downhill. But I decided to leave the past behind. We were dealing with his grief, and I didn't want to bring up mine.

"Well ..." His glistening eyes grew wider. "Sometimes, when you least expect it, something amazing comes along." He opened his palm and wiped away the remaining sand off something white, about four inches long.

"A seashell," I exclaimed. One that looked just like the one I had found.

"Once in a while, a seashell washes up the shore, but I've never seen this kind here. Usually, I find sand dollars, shark eyes, a sunray venus, or ..." He stopped when I eyed him suspiciously. "I promise I'm not some kind of seashell geek, or you'll never date me. I mean, you won't hang out with me." He chuckled. "When you live on the beach, it's inevitable to be curious about the seashells you find."

"Don't worry," I said. "Because if you were a true seashell geek, then you would know the name of this one. Recently, I found a similar one, only a bit bigger. Kate told me it's called an angel wing."

He looked at the seashell, contemplating. "Here. It's yours now."

"Wait." I held out a hand.

I knew what I was about to tell him was stretching it, but he needed a reminder that his mother loved him and that she wouldn't hold anything against him for not being there when he thought she'd needed him. I wasn't his mother, but that was what I would want for Tyler.

I bit my bottom lip. "This might sound strange, but I was told that the person who finds an angel wing is meant to keep it. We've been talking about your mother, and I think it's a sign from her. She loves you and wants you to live your life without guilt."

I had made up the part about the person who found the angel wing was meant to keep it, but it felt right. Stories had to start somewhere.

Ian's gaze pierced into mine with intensity. I'd thought he was going to tell me I was wrong or that I had no right to speak for his mother, but instead, his eyes became glassy under the pale moonlight. Perhaps he was holding back tears.

"You think so?" He sounded uncertain, but it also sounded like he needed to hear it.

"Yes." I cupped my hands over his so he wouldn't hand me the seashell. "Keep it in your room, somewhere safe, as a reminder."

Ian nodded somberly, then looked thoughtful. "I have a confession to make. I *am* somewhat of a seashell geek. I knew it was called an angel wing because my mother told me. She also told me a myth to go with them."

"Interesting. How does it go?"

Ian peered up to the sky. "An angel fell in love with a human. He loved her so much that he asked if he could turn into a mortal to be with her. When he was denied, he was so heartbroken that he dove into the ocean. When his wings touched the water, each feather turned into an angel wing seashell so that we would be reminded that love conquers all. And even when our loved ones are gone, they'll always be in our hearts, in our memories, and in everything they leave behind. A reminder that love never dies."

My heart skipped a beat. "It's a beautiful myth. Thank you for sharing it with me."

"Also, I think you're right that the person who finds an angel wing is meant to have it. This type of seashell is found from West Indies to Brazil, Cape Cod to the Gulf of Mexico. It lives in shallow water and sometimes three feet deep in the mud. So, for one to grace us with its presence is incredible."

"I couldn't agree with you more."

"And you said you found one recently? Two at the same island? Must be fate." His lips tugged at the corners, and he offered his hand. "I suppose fate brought you and Kate to Kauai, of all places. Lee and I have to thank either an angel or someone looking after us. Meeting genuine, kindhearted people is hard to do these days."

I dusted sand off my bottom, then off my hands. "Kate and I are thankful to have met the both of you, too."

"Well, I wouldn't say that too quickly, Abby. You haven't met the real me yet. Did you bring an extra change of clothes?"

"No," I said hesitantly, wondering why he would ask.

"That's okay. You can wear mine."

I narrowed my eyes. "What do you mean?"

Quick as a wink, Ian took off his T-shirt. "We have the best view. Let's not let this go to waste. This is the best time to swim. You're going to love it. Trust me."

Swim? Before I could process his words, he hoisted me into his arms. I swallowed a breath and wrapped my arms around his neck as he ran toward the ocean.

"Ian!" I hollered.

Trust me. I did trust him, so I stopped kicking and surrendered.

Chapter Eighteen — Bucket List

"**I**an!" I screamed.

I'd thought he would stop when water touched our feet, but we submerged into the freezing water, me still in his arms. Shocked by the change in temperature, I shivered until my teeth chattered.

"You're c-c-crazy."

Ian let out a belly laugh. "Let me warm you up. I'm going to let go."

My toes sank into the sand, and water rose to my shoulder blades. I gasped, too cold to shriek. Just when I thought hypothermia was about to set in, Ian gathered me in his arms, and together we jumped the waves, letting the water buoy our leaps.

"There. Better?" He pulled back.

My body adjusted to the temperature, and it wasn't as cold. Ian was right. Here. In the darkness. Just the two of us under the gorgeous moonlit sky, I could paint this. This view. This moment. But this feeling … My heart hadn't settled back after its leap into the stars, yet.

I felt so small in the vast universe, in the endless dark sea. In a way, it was terrifying, but so tranquil. As if only the two of us existed and time was irrelevant. No pain. No suffering. No guilt. Just pure bliss. At one with myself and this amazing man in front of me.

"Was I right, Abby? Isn't this the best?" Ian raked his wet hair back, looking like a water god, resurfacing to rescue me.

I needed to stop reading those fantasy books.

"It is." I swayed with the water's irresistible pull. "I've never gone night swimming before."

"Then we'll have to see what other things you haven't done and do them. Do you have a bucket list? It's okay if you don't. Not everyone does."

I spread my fingers and tapped the undulating surface of the water with my palms to avert my eyes. That close, his dazzling smile was bright as the moon, shaming the curtain of stars spread behind him.

Sure, we were getting to know each other as friends, but my God, did he have to be so distractingly attractive, with a bonus amazing personality? He was one hell of a package.

"As a matter of fact, I do," I said. "The list isn't long, though."

Ian ran his fingers through his hair again, water dripping down his face. I wished he would stop doing that.

"That's okay. You can keep adding to it. No list is ever final."

"True." I hopped with a wave pushing through and fluttered my hand under the water.

"I'll share one of mine if you share one of yours." He narrowed his eyes, daring me.

"You first."

He chuckled, the rumbling sound pleasant and light. "My list is long, but one of them is skydiving. It's at the very bottom of the *maybe* list."

"What? You can't have a *maybe* list. There's no such thing." I laughed.

"Why not? It's my list. There's no rule on how you create a bucket list. How about yours?"

I shifted sand under my feet. "One of them is zip-lining."

"That's a fun one. You'll love it."

"I don't know. I'm afraid of heights. I should put that on my *maybe* list."

Ian narrowed his eyes. "Remember, there's no such thing as a maybe list. A wise, beautiful woman told me so, and I must listen."

I snorted and fought the urge to swim away from his compliment.

"Anyway, there's a place I know," he continued. "It's not *too* high, and I promise you'll love it. We should go next weekend. We can invite the whole gang. How about it?"

Before I could chicken out, I said, "Let's do it."

Tyler had been asking to go zip lining, but I had no interest, thinking it was too dangerous for the both of us. I knew I was being overcautious, but I'd rather be safe than sorry. Regarding my son, I had to do everything in my power to protect him. Even if it was giving up a little fun. God knows, life was unpredictable. I needed to control what I could. But with Ian asking me to go with the gang, I became emboldened.

"Great. I'll make the arrangements." Ian's eyes grew wider. "Abby, hold my hand. There's a big wave coming. I'll guide you. Jump when I tell you."

I glanced over my shoulder toward the sea. A giant wave was just starting to break, and my heart hammered against my chest. *Oh, God. Oh, God.* I knew how to swim, but anyone who lived in Hawaii knew that even experienced swimmers could get caught.

My mind reeled with bleak scenarios of me drowning and Tyler growing up without either of his parents. I bobbed nervously. I didn't like the feeling of sand pulling me deeper into the ocean. Panic rose in my throat. I was going to be sucked under with the current and never rise.

"One. Two. Now, as high as you can, Abby," Ian directed. "Jump."

I pushed off on my toes, Ian's vise grip locked on mine—a promise he would never let go—and raised me with him. The swelling wave caught and lifted us, and we passed through. To my surprise, I enjoyed it.

Ian wiped the water off his face and chuckled. "That wasn't so bad, right?"

A joyful noise escaped my throat. "That was actually fun. I can cross this one off my bucket list."

Ian stared at me incredulously. "You've never jumped over a wave before? You used to live in LA. You have a beach."

"It's just that I hate the feeling when the water and the sand flow out and pull me toward the deeper water. It terrifies me."

"And yet here you are," he said softly. His eyes roamed my face.

"I bet you're not afraid of anything." I craned my neck to check for another wave.

He tilted his head back, his lips slowly curving upward. "You'd be surprised, but I'm kind of afraid of horses. I've never been horseback riding."

I blinked, incredulous. "Horseback riding. Are you pulling my leg? I don't believe you."

For someone from a wealthy family, a man who seemed to have experienced many things, it didn't seem possible.

He raised his hands. "I promise to the moon and the stars, the universe, or whoever you want me to swear to, but I've never been horseback riding. My mother was very protective, especially about horses. And understandably so. One of her good friends fell off a horse during a ride when they were kids. Broke her spine and became quadriplegic."

"Oh ..." I slapped my mouth. "I'm so sorry."

"But I still would like to ride one day. It's on my bucket list. Have you?"

"I took Tyler last year for the first time. We went on a short trail with an instructor, so it was very safe. Well, as safe as possible."

"Did he ride on a pony?"

"Yes. So how about we make a deal. You can take me zip-lining, and I'll take you horseback riding."

"It depends."

I frowned and hardened my features. "Depends on what?"

"Do you think they'll let me ride a pony?" He waggled his brows playfully.

I let out a belly laugh, almost sucking in water.

"Hey, that's not funny." Ian's lips turned downward in a pout. "I mean it. You have to go slow with me."

Water splattered my face, and I blinked. There was no wave like the last time, only the gentle tide. Then it dawned on me.

"Did you just splash me?" I shrieked and didn't give him a chance to answer as I smacked the water toward him.

He ran a hand down his face. "And she fights back." His expression darkened with mischief.

Oh, crap! Predicting his next move, I pushed sheets of water at Ian as he water-bombed me right back. We were acting like children, but I didn't care. Nobody could see us.

I craned my neck away from his assaults, slapping at the ocean, laughing and laughing. It had been a while since I had laughed that hard. My sides ached, and my throat grew sore with screams and coughs in the salty spray. Ian was having a blast, too. Then his eyes grew wide.

"Oh, shit, Abby!"

Ian reached for me, but he couldn't get to me fast enough. We had backed away from each other during the water fight. There was nothing dangerous about this situation. I had my feet solid on the ground. But the wave coming at us was double the size of the previous one, and I lost my courage.

When I was younger, I had been hit by a large wave that had not only taken me under but held me prisoner in its tumble. That wave, that childhood terror was the reason playing in the surf made me anxious.

I froze and clasped my hands under my chin. Ian glimpsed my expression and grew serious.

"Abby, go down as far as you can, all the way down. I'll find you."

I trusted him. Without hesitation, I sucked in a lung full of air and dropped as far as I could. Just as the water slammed into me, Ian wrapped his arms and legs around me like a net.

We somersaulted and toppled sideways, and the next thing I knew, we flopped, my back on the sand and Ian on top of me. Both of our chests heaved, breaths colliding together.

Ian pushed my hair away from my face. "Are you okay?"

Oh, God. The rush from the danger. His body over me, one leg between mine in an intimate way. My breath caught.

"That was wild and fun. I can't believe I'm not freaking out. Getting slammed by a giant wave was never on my bucket list, but I'm going to put it on the top of my list and check it off."

Ian plopped next to me and chuckled. "I never landed on top of anyone in the water before. Bucket list. Check."

I turned to him, water lapping by my feet. "Is that allowed? Adding something to the bucket list *after* we do it?"

His eyes gleamed under the silver moon and the stars. The slow curve of his full lips, and the way his knuckle caressed my cheek—warmth spread through my body. The magic of the moment drove away all thoughts as my pulse quickened, reminding me I was alive. Not just a mother but a woman.

Friends. We're friends. But can two single people be friends? Yes, they can. I'd had guy friends in college, but those friendships had dissipated after Steve and I became a couple. *This is different.*

I shivered. The adrenaline pumping through me had kept me warm, or at least oblivious, but the wind chilled my wet limbs once the ocean no longer had me in its cocoon.

Ian jerked his hand back, as if finally realizing what he was doing. It seemed we were both victims of this magical night.

"We should go before you catch a cold." Ian offered his hand, and I took it.

I dragged my wet feet across the sand, my limbs trembling. We gathered our stuff, and Ian tossed the blanket around us.

"So, here's our story," he said. "You fell in the water, and when I tried to help you, you pulled me in."

"What?" I snorted. "They're not going to believe you."

"Come on, Abby. We're a team." Ian's voice dipped playfully. "Or I can tell them that we went skinny dipping."

"What?" I laughed harder. "They'll never believe you. Our clothes are wet. But, fine. I'll take the first excuse."

Ian opened the double glass door, and I tried to tiptoe inside without noticing, but all heads turned toward us. Tyler blinked, looking confused, while every other adult's mouth fell open. Heat rushed up to my neck, warming my every inch.

They hadn't moved. They were still playing video games on the big screen and lounging on the sofa.

"Are you two okay?" Lee asked hesitantly.

"Yeah," Ian said nonchalantly. "We were talking and got too close to the water. A huge wave crashed over us."

My sister perked her lips as if she was trying to hold in a laugh. Stella and Isaac quirked their eyebrows.

"Anyway, get back to whatever you were doing." Ian guided me toward the hall. "I'm going to take Abby to the restroom so we can take a shower. I mean, not together. Separate."

I didn't think I could blush any harder, but my face flamed so hot, my eyes watered. *Blimey.*

Ian guided me around the corner and passed the foyer to the other side, then three bedrooms. The last one was his. Ian's bedroom was double the size of mine.

A sofa rested by the window, across from a large TV. The furniture was modern, and the room was simply designed. No paintings hung, and no photos were laid out on his dresser.

Ian opened his walk-in closet and brought out a beige bath towel and some other things on top of it.

"The sweatpants and the T-shirt should fit you." He laid them on the bed. "I hope you don't mind wearing some of my sister's stuff. They're new."

"Are you sure?" I asked. "Then I'll just buy her a new one."

"It's not necessary. She has plenty, so don't worry about it. And behind you is the bathroom. I'm going to take a shower in the other room." Ian halted by the door and turned, giving me that gorgeous smile. "Thank you for a wonderful evening, Abby. Thanks for being a friend.

It meant a lot to me. And I want you to know that I'm here for you."

I didn't know what to say. It had been a long time since I laughed so much that I had teared up. Maybe I didn't need to make a big speech. Perhaps something simple would suffice.

"You're welcome, Ian." I gave him my best smile.

"Oh, I almost forgot." He reached inside his front pocket and pulled out the seashell. "I thought I lost it when we went under water." He went to the table by his bed, set it by the lamp, and then shut the door behind him.

I smiled at the little angel wing seashell. Somehow the little trinket stood out from the room as if it was the most precious thing. After I grabbed the towel and change of clothes, I stepped onto the white marble floor. I stacked the clothes on a marble-topped vanity with a mirror that lit up in a circle.

The standalone porcelain bathtub had a gorgeous view of the beach. I imagined taking a bubble bath with a glass of wine, lighting candles around the tub, and enjoying the sunset.

After I stripped off my wet clothes, I stepped into the shower. My feet rested on slightly curved tiles that collectively created one big lavender orchid. There were two waterspouts from each end, and a place where you could sit. When I lathered up the soap, I smelled like Ian—musky, mixed with ocean breeze.

I shouldn't smell like Ian. No, no, no. I should smell like Steve.

What did Steve smell like? I had forgotten. I couldn't forget. This wasn't right. Guilt tore through me. I *had* to remember. Had to ... had to remember.

The warm water felt hotter as my pulse hammered. I planted a hand on the glass door and let the water pour over my body. *Think. Think. Think.* I shoved my palms to my face, nearly in tears.

Steve smelled ... he smelled like ... coffee. Yes. Coffee. He loved coffee.

I let out a strange laughing sound, happy to recall. So happy I hadn't forgotten a simple memory. I couldn't forget.

When Tyler and I got home, he lay on my bed next to me. I took in the rare, precious moment and counted my blessings.

"Did you have a good time tonight?" I asked.

Tyler shifted on his side and tucked his hands under the pillow. "I had so much fun. Ian, Isaac, and Lee are so cool. They're like big kids."

I snuggled closer. "Even adults need to have fun, too. And sometimes that requires acting like children."

His grin widened. "I like it when they play video games with me."

I stroked my son's soft hair. Sometimes when he smiled, I could see my softer features in him.

"I bet you do." I tapped his nose. "Did you finish your weekend homework?"

"I'm all done." Tyler pinched his eyebrows to the center, seemingly deep in thought as the silence grew between us. He opened his mouth to talk but then shut it instead.

"Tyler. Do you want to tell me something?"

He squinted, scrunching his nose. He rolled to his back and gazed at the ceiling, his shoulders tense. The light from the lamp shadowed half his face, and it became harder to see his expression.

"Ty. What's wrong, sweetheart? You know you can tell me anything."

No matter how busy I was at work, I made an effort to talk to Tyler daily when we ate dinner together. I'd ask him how his day was, about his friends, and anything he was willing to share.

Being a parent—especially a single parent—was difficult and rewarding in almost equal measure. He used to chatter away about his friends or whatever childish thought occupied him. But the older Tyler got, the harder it was to get him to talk about his feelings or concerns. I had my sister to talk things through, and my parents, but Tyler had only me.

"I know, Mom. But this is …" He released a long sigh.

I propped up against the pillow and reached out to him, but he didn't take my hand. "Did I do something wrong? Did I hurt your feelings?"

He shook his head. "It's just that … I don't know …"

"I promise you won't hurt my feelings. Remember, I can't read your mind, Ty. We have to work things through."

As my thoughts went in a hundred different directions, I remained patient. It wasn't about his schoolwork. He excelled in all of his subjects. I tried to think of any new changes lately, but came up empty. Ian?

He sat up and faced me, the strain on his forehead easing. "We talked about this before, but I don't remember Dad much. I see his picture every day in my room, but it's just a photo. I sort of remember him playing ball with me, but that's all."

I caressed his hair again. "It's okay, sweetheart. You were so young. That's why I put a picture of your father in your room—so you wouldn't forget him."

Like how I had almost forgotten what Steve smelled like. I understood his frustration, but Tyler's situation was understandable. Inevitable, really. But for me? Unforgivable. Over time, I might forget more about my husband. And this frightened me.

He lowered his gaze to his fingers, gripping the blanket. "There's going to be a father and son miniature golfing event at our school." He bobbed his shoulders. "I guess I can't go."

I smoothed my hand over the covers, repeating the action as I thought. Did he want me to console him? I started and discarded several beginnings.

"Can a mother go instead of a father?" I finally said.

He met my gaze and shrugged. "I don't know, but that would be weird."

I didn't think so, but Tyler liked to stick to the rules. He was so by-the-book, like me in that sense. Surely if I spoke to his teacher or the event coordinator, they would make exceptions. But Tyler might get mad at me for asking.

"How about if I ask Lee to take you?" I didn't want to put Lee in an awkward situation, but he would say yes in a heartbeat. Tyler had practically become his nephew, and would be when Lee proposed to Kate.

Tyler pushed his leg out and touched my toes with his foot. When he was little, he used to compare his feet to mine. He always giggled when I told him that his feet would be bigger one day. When that day came, I knew I'd cry.

Tyler looked pensive, his nose scrunching. "Is Ian going to be my dad?"

Surprised by his question, I hesitated. "No. What gave you that idea?"

But I knew. I had seen Tyler's face when Ian and I walked in from the beach, smiling and soaked head to toe. Tyler had seen Ian kiss my cheek, and he might have even picked up on the other adults' teasing.

He flopped onto his back. "Ian picked me up when you were sick, and we see him a lot. He's nice to me, and I like him. Can we ask him to take me to the father and son event?"

Ian was the first man besides Lee to be welcomed into my home.

Tyler was getting the wrong idea. This was the reason I had to be careful.

"Ty." I took his hand in mine. "Ian is my friend. And I don't think it's a good idea if we ask him to take you."

"Why?" He blinked, his voice soft.

Just when I'd thought the dagger couldn't cut any deeper, he looked at me with those innocent, sorrowful eyes.

"Because he's not your father." It took effort to calm my nerves. The anger surprised me—not at my son, but at the world and the unfairness of life.

Sure, other kids had it worse, and we had plenty of blessings, but no mother liked seeing their child hurt. We had our health and each other, but that wasn't always enough for a kid wanting his father.

He scowled at the ceiling, then his frown cleared as he slid off the bed. "I'm going to go to bed now. I'm tired."

"Do you want to talk more about it?"

"Nah." He dipped his head. "I just won't go. All my friends know I don't have a father, anyway."

And just like that, he was willing to let it go. Troubles were out the door. Tyler was flexible and easygoing, but he still looked unhappy. Perhaps I was reading too much into it. I wanted to protect him, protect his heart. I wanted him to be happy.

"Ty ..." I scooted to the edge of the bed, holding back tears. "I'm very proud of you for being strong and for understanding. I know you wish you had a father like all your friends, but life isn't the same for everyone. I told you that many times, remember?"

"Yeah. Lee told me that just because I don't have a father doesn't mean I'm different than anyone else. An uncle or a friend can be a role model, too. Lee said he would always be there for me if I needed someone else besides you or Auntie Kate."

Oh, Lee. Bless his heart.

Tyler added, "And Ian told me that if I ever needed anything, he would be there for me, too."

"He did?" My pitch rose.

Ian was like a brother to Lee. And Ian knew that Lee was planning to propose to Kate, but that didn't mean he had to treat Tyler like family, too. Regardless of his motive, I appreciated his thoughtfulness. I hoped it wasn't a false promise, and I hoped his kindness to my son didn't depend on my choices. I didn't know Ian that well, but he had shown me he was a good man, so far.

"I'm going to sleep now. Goodnight, Mom."

"Hey ..." I got off the bed and hugged him. "Where's my kiss?"

He wrapped his arms around me and planted a quick peck on my cheek. "I love you across the galaxies and beyond, Mom. You're the best mom in the whole wide world."

This boy was my life. "I love you even *beyond* beyond."

That had been Steve's special way of telling Tyler that he loved him. Tyler didn't remember, of course, but I had told him about it often, so he wouldn't forget that his dad had loved him fiercely. In a way, the quirky phrase reassured Tyler that no matter where his father was, in this world or beyond, his love for him would be forever.

"Oh, Ty," I said as he passed through the door.

He spun.

"Ian wants to take us zip-lining and horseback riding. What do you think about that?"

His mouth opened wide, then he punched his fist into the air. "Yes! Finally. I can't wait."

Chapter Twenty — Shopping

I dropped Tyler at Lee's place and headed to the local outdoor mall with Stella and Kate. It had been months since I'd gone shopping, and I had to admit, I felt giddy.

Cottony clouds adorned the beautiful sky, and the warm sun bathed my skin. Just the right amount of flower-scented breeze kept the weather from being too hot as we went from store to store. No luck in finding that perfect dress, so far, for the auction, until we went inside a little boutique.

"What do you think?" I held up a knee-length spaghetti-strapped black dress. The fabric would lay over my curves but wouldn't hug tight. A satiny underlayer was covered in lace.

"That's going to look nice on you," Kate said and pulled out a black dress similar to mine, though strapless and without the lace.

Kate was a little more daring than me. I wouldn't be caught dead wearing anything strapless.

"Are you both going to a funeral?" Stella giggled. "All these colorful dresses, and you go for black?" She flipped through the circular rack, pulled out a silk dress, and placed it in front of her.

"Beautiful. Red looks good on you," I said.

Stella shrugged sheepishly in a shy way that was uncharacteristic of her. Then she turned back to the rack. Kate tugged my arm and moved toward the dressing room.

Kate leaned closer to me, keeping an eye on Stella. "So, Lee told me we're all going zip-lining and horseback riding. I didn't know if Stella and Isaac were invited, so I wanted to check before saying anything."

I shifted the hangers on the rack, searching. "I don't know what's going on between Stella and Isaac. Besides, it wouldn't be fun for them, anyway. We're accommodating the event around Tyler and Bridget."

Kate took a red dress off the rack, compared it to the black one she held, and then put the red one back. "You're afraid of heights. And you wouldn't go zip-lining with your own sister. How in the world did Ian convince you to go?" Her tone was sharp, as if something offended her.

I flashed her an apologetic look. "We were talking about our bucket lists."

"What?" She said it louder than she'd intended. Stella, about five racks down, narrowed her eyes at us.

Kate cleared her throat and ran fingers through her hair, embarrassed. She leaned in closer. "You have a bucket list? When? How come you never told me about it?"

"Well …" I scrunched my features. "I didn't have one, and I kind of made one up when Ian asked me about it. I thought about what I *would* have put on my bucket list if I ever wrote it down. But it was in my head already, so I didn't lie about it."

Kate snickered. "You crack me up."

"What's so funny?" I elbowed her arm lightly.

"Nothing." Kate nodded at Stella coming toward us with five dresses. "Someone knows how to pick them."

"So, do you think something is up with Isaac and Stella?" I asked quickly.

"Why don't you ask her?" There was a challenge in her voice.

"No way. It's none of my business."

Stella glanced at Kate and me and frowned. "Both of you still have only one."

"Must not be a good shopping day for us," I said. "Shall we go to the dressing room?"

Stella pivoted and led the way. Just as we went to our individual dressing rooms, Stella looked over her shoulder and said, "Oh, I forgot. Isaac told me to say hello. And if you're wondering about Isaac and me, we're going on our first date soon."

"What? When?" I grabbed Stella's arm.

"Isaac asked me out at the beach house." Her smile widened. "He's taking me out to dinner tomorrow night."

Stella had dated someone for a long time, but they'd broken up when she'd graduated from college. That was all Kate and I knew about her relationship. She didn't talk about her love life, and we never asked.

We modeled the dresses for each other, and Kate and I both went with the dresses we'd first picked out. On our way to the food court, I stopped at the children's store and bought Tyler a pair of jeans. While we ate, I brought up work, even though I had told myself I wouldn't. But we had to decide on who to hire, and I wanted whoever we chose to start right away.

We'd held the last of the interviews the day before, and we'd narrowed the choices down to two candidates: Liam and Cecelia, who Kate had interviewed. Her résumé was impressive, however, I hadn't gotten a chance to meet her in person.

"So, Liam or Cecelia?" Kate bit into a hard-shell taco, holding her hand underneath as it crumbled.

Stella's straw popped out of her mouth. "Liam. Definitely."

I glared at her. "You want Liam because you think he's cute."

"I do not." Stella snorted, twirling chow mein noodles with her chopsticks. "I'm dating Isaac now, remember?" She raised her chin as if she'd just said she was dating a king.

"Well ..." Kate forked up corn and strips of lettuce that fell from her taco. She looked pensive, her eyes on her plate.

"You going to make us guess?" Stella said in her usually light but sarcastic tone.

"Oh, sorry." Kate shook her head. "I was thinking about the two candidates. They're both strong, but have different strengths, and Abby and I are sort of biased toward the one we interviewed, as they both made a good impression. This is so hard." She blew out a breath.

I pointed at my sister's forehead and perked my lips, trying not to laugh. "You got guacamole on your face."

She wiped with a napkin and tilted her forehead toward me. "Is it gone?"

I smeared the morsel she hadn't caught. My sister was always getting paint on herself, on her clothes, and also making a mess while eating. We made a good pair, as I tried to be tidy and well organized.

"We're getting off-topic," Stella whined. "I looked all through their websites, and I also snooped around their social media."

"You did?" I took a spoonful of rice and beef.

Some companies went through interviewees' social media sites to check if they were political or had any red flags. I couldn't do it, but I had thought about it. Personal lives were none of my business. But I also had to think of the gallery's reputation and the group dynamics, so I was thankful Stella had done it.

Stella waggled her eyebrows. "They're both fine. But ..." She held up a finger. "Liam has a decent-sized platform and engaged followers. They love his style. We can put him in charge of social media sites. My followers are basically my friends and family, but Liam's followers are art fanatics from all over the world."

"I agree with Stella," Kate said. "Let's hire Liam."

"Then that settles it. I'll call him first thing Monday morning." I picked up my drink and gulped iced tea, glad to settle the issue.

My phone buzzed. My heart leaped as thoughts of something bad happening to Tyler rushed to my mind. Lee was watching him. My son was fine, I reminded myself.

The text wasn't from Lee, but Ian. He sent me a photo of Tyler, Lee, Bridget, and himself. Seeing the four of them warmed my heart.

"Look. How cute is this?" I flipped my phone to show Kate and Stella.

"Awww. That's ... Wait." Stella narrowed her eyes. "Who sent it to you?"

I suddenly felt self-conscious. I flipped the phone back over and said, "Ian."

I should have lied. Stella's eyebrows raised so high her eyeballs almost popped out. I leaned back and continued eating. But Stella and Kate exchanged glances. My face burned hot red at the thought. I slid my phone into my lap and texted Ian.

Abby: Thank you for this picture. I love it.

Ian: I thought it would make your day.

He had been making many of my days, lately. I put away my phone and ignored the others.

Chapter Twenty~One — Zip~Lining

K ate, Lee, and Bridget took one car while Ian picked up Tyler and me from my house. We met at the Skyline Kauai office. The instructors, Tim and Kevin, introduced themselves and went over the rules and what to expect. Then we tried on helmets. The children were practically hopping in their excitement.

Lee clapped his hands once. "Are you ready to have fun?" he asked the kids.

"This is my first time." Tyler pointed at me. "Mom wouldn't let me, before, and she was afraid something would happen."

Lee bent lower and tapped Tyler's helmet. "I know. We're going on the easy one. This will be Bridget's first time, too. You're both going to love it."

"I don't know about my mom. She's afraid of heights." Tyler patted my back as if he was the parent consoling his child.

Who was acting like the adult here? I almost laughed.

"Your mom will be fine. I promise." Ian massaged Tyler's shoulder with one hand and then mine with his other.

I gave Ian a nervous smile. His sly grin made my heart speed up, but it had the double effect of making me less nervous about the zip line.

"Come on, sis." Kate swung her arm around me, leading me out the glass doors behind the instructor. "The zip-lining course is a little hike up the hill. The first time might be scary, but afterward, you'll be begging for more."

I raised an eyebrow and leaned closer so only she could hear. "Sounds like what our cousin Susan told us about sex."

Kate burst out laughing. When I had been a junior in high school and Kate a freshman, our cousin had told us *all* about losing her virginity to her boyfriend, and their sex life.

My sister and I had been horrified and intrigued.

Kate readjusted her camera bag over her shoulder. "I still recall the expression on your face, like the one you have now."

I snorted. "You know how scared I am of heights. I can't even climb a ladder."

"I know, but I promise you'll love it." She tapped my helmet.

"I better, or someone is going to owe me big time."

My tennis shoe scuffed on the dirt path, then I stepped on a walkway of dead grass. A few dandelions had sprouted alongside the track. I looked over my shoulder. Tyler and Bridget were walking between Lee and Ian.

"This was your idea, remember?" Kate reminded me.

"No, I believe it was Ian's."

Kate had wanted to take me zip-lining, but I had turned her down every time. I didn't see the point of going when I knew I'd turn right back and go home as soon as I set foot in the place. But zip-lining was on my bucket list, and I guessed I needed a good reason to take that plunge. Besides, I wanted to be the one to give my son his first zip-lining experience. I wanted him to remember that we'd gone together.

Grassy hills surrounded our group with patches of darker green and dried areas. That unique island scent of saltwater and lush tropical plants surrounded me with a sense of calm. Palm trees stood tall among hedges and thickets, their fronds bobbing in the wind. The clouds foamed over the rolling mountains like whipped cream on an ice cream sundae.

This view wasn't anything spectacular, not even unusual in Kauai, but it felt like it was the first time I'd seen it. Perhaps new experiences threw familiar things into a new light.

"Here we are." Tim grinned, bouncing on the balls of his feet like a kid at a toy store. "Kevin is on the other side. Everyone wave to him. He'll be the one to catch you. Are you ready?"

"Yes," collective voices said with enthusiasm.

No, I screamed in my mind.

Tim demonstrated how to sit and where to hold. "Now, who's going first?"

Tyler raised his hand.

"Let's have an adult go first, and then Tyler can go next. Sound good?" Tim gave a thumbs up to my son.

Kate took pictures while Lee strapped himself in and soared across effortlessly. Afterward, Tyler went, then Bridget. Kate clicked away on her camera again. Tyler didn't show an ounce of fear, but Bridget screamed.

Kevin was there to bring her in when she got to the other side. Bridget and Tyler jumped up and down while they waved.

"See you on the other side, sis." Kate gave me a salute and sailed smoothly across a short distance, her camera bag snugged tightly in front of her sling.

"Abby, do you want to go next?" Ian asked, his voice tender. "I would go with you, but it's only one person at a time."

I blew out a slow breath and nodded. "You go first. I need a little more time."

He gave me a pat on my back. "You can do this."

I shook my hands and rubbed my legs. Ian cupped my face, forcing me to look at those gorgeous dark eyes that appeared lighter in the sunlight.

"Abby, I promise you're going to love it. Keep your eyes focused on one spot ahead of you. Maybe on Tyler, if you want. Just don't look down. After it's done, you can check it off your bucket list. Then we can celebrate."

"Okay," I said, trying to sound positive, giving him my best smile.

I watched Ian lock the straps around himself. He waved at me and sailed effortlessly. In fact, this course was a joke for the grownups. But I appreciated Lee, Kate, and Ian for being good sports and accommodating.

You've got this. Your family is waiting for you on the other side.

"Ready, Abby?" Tim asked. The sun highlighted the tips of his dirty-blond hair.

I walked toward Tim's extended hand, and when my feet met the wooden planks, I slowed.

"Your first time?" Tim asked.

"Yes." My palms felt clammy, and my knees wobbled.

"First time is the hardest. I've had countless customers, so you're in good hands, okay?" His calming voice reassured me, but when I looked out, my heart pounded.

I swallowed and sat on the harness, allowing Tim to lock me in place.

"Hold on to these bars and either keep your knees bent or your legs straight out. I'm going to give you a little push. Just fly with the wind."

Focus on Tyler. Don't look down. It's going to be fine.

From the other side, Kate took pictures of me while everyone clapped and shouted words of encouragement.

"Here we go. Get ready." Tim brought me closer to the point of no return, and my heart somersaulted down to my stomach. All my nerve endings froze, locking my fingers around the bar holding me in place. No way would that harness hold me up. I wanted to vomit.

THE SEASHELL OF 'OHANA

Oh, God. Oh, God. Oh, God. Whose crazy idea was this? Why had I opened up to Ian and let him talk me into going zip-lining? For goodness' sake, I didn't even have a bucket list. It only counts if you write it down, right?

"On the count of three, Abby. One … Two …"

I thought about backing out. My breaths grew shallow and fast. No, I couldn't. I didn't want Tyler to think less of his mother, and I certainly didn't want to disappoint Ian, who was shouting my name.

"Three …"

My body went rigid. All reasonable expectations of "everything will be fine" were tossed into the breeze. I tightened my hold on the bar as if it were my lifeline, and Tim's push from behind shot me off the platform. As soon as my feet dangled in the air, my stomach dropped to the planet below, and I screamed, my throat raw.

The blue sky and cotton-like clouds seemed an arm's length away, and the evergreen trees and the terrain welcomed me with open arms. *Don't look down,* Tim had said, but that was the thing about being in an open space—it was nearly impossible not to.

Halfway across, my fear resolved as fast as it had come. I was the little bird afraid to jump, but once I spread my wings, I flew. I became one with the wind and the earth. Serenity filled my soul.

I felt small yet grand, and I laughed from the sheer joy of it. I was high. Ecstatic. And I wanted more. At that moment, I thought of Steve. We were supposed to zip line together. He'd wanted to be the one to take me first.

I'm flying, Steve. I wish I could fly to where you are. And if he were here, he would say, "You're doing great, Abby. I'm so proud of you."

When I neared the stop, Kevin had his feet planted, his arms stretched out, ready for me while everyone stood to the side, waiting for my reaction.

I yelped and gasped when the cable braked. As soon as Kevin released me, I released the harness. My knees buckled.

"Abby." Ian came to me with open arms, his features marred with concern.

As soon as his warm, secure embrace enveloped me, tears trickled down my face, and I sobbed softly. I had no idea why I was crying. Maybe it was the pride and relief of conquering my fear. Maybe it was that I had done this without Steve.

Tyler wrapped his arms around me from behind, and the three of us stood there. If Steve were here, we would be doing this exact thing.

But Ian wasn't Steve, so I backed away and wiped my eyes.

"I'm so sorry." I sniffed as I looked at the worried faces around me.

Kate looked horrified, and Tyler's eyes were wide and unblinking.

"I'm so sorry, Abby." Ian reached out for me, but he pulled back and shoved his hands in his pockets. "I shouldn't have—"

I didn't want him to feel guilty, especially when he'd done nothing wrong.

"I don't know what's the matter with me," I said. "I have to admit, I was terrified, but I love it. Can we do it again?"

Their somber expression turned to happy ones.

"I knew it." Ian hugged me and swung me around.

When my feet touched the ground, Tyler grabbed my arm.

"You liked it, Mom? You really liked it?" Tyler's excited voice rang in the air.

"Yes." I cupped his face and kissed his cheek. "Did you?"

"I did. It was the best. But are you sure you're okay?"

My son's concern filled me with joy. He even held my hand, which he rarely ever did these days. Tim came from the other side, and we continued with the tour.

At every stop, the course went higher and higher, but there was a limit on the height for the beginner's course. Every time it was my turn, I reveled in the feeling of flight, as mesmerized as the first time. Afterward, we went to a local diner to eat lunch.

While we waited for our meal, Kate pulled out her camera and scrolled through the photos she'd taken. She'd gotten a shot of Ian, Tyler, and I huddled together as if we were a family. My throat tightened.

Steve should have been the one in the photo.

Chapter Twenty-Two — Liam

All the parking spaces at Tyler's school were taken. Most of the parked cars belonged to kindergarten parents walking their kids to the gate to wait for their teachers. I had no choice but to drive to the drop-off curb, which also meant I had to get in the slow-moving line of cars.

I missed Tyler being five. I recalled the first day I'd brought him to this school. He'd had on his *Skeletons versus Unicorns* backpack with a matching lunchbox. Bridget had, too. They had the same teacher. Tyler had hardly slept the night before from excitement.

As I waited for the car ahead of me to drive off, a huge banner displayed at the front of the school caught my eyes—Father-Son *Miniature Golf Event*. Guilt took a space in my heart.

I thought again about asking his teacher if a mother could go instead, but Tyler wouldn't want that. I hoped I was making the right decision. It was difficult being a single parent. Father-son events cut twice, once for the parent he'd lost and again for the little ways the world reminded him he didn't have a dad. I wanted my son to have all the experiences and not be left out.

"Have the best day, Ty," I said. "I love you across the galaxies and beyond."

Tyler checked the button on his Polo top and dusted something off his new pair of jeans I had bought when I'd gone shopping with Kate and Stella. He looked sleek and ready to conquer schoolwork. I was so proud of him.

"I love you across the galaxies and beyond, too," he said quickly, his words jumbled together.

He flashed me a grin with all his teeth and pushed through the door with his backpack. I should have driven off, but I waited to watch him greet his friend and walk through the gates.

Impatient honking from behind startled me. I looked in the rearview mirror to see Jessica Conner, a blue-eyed auburn behind the wheel of a silver Mercedes-Benz. I frowned.

Jessica was polite to me when she felt like it, but she came off as rude and pretentious to others.

"Hi, Abby," Jessica shouted, her head out the window, waving frantically. "I didn't know it was you, or I wouldn't have honked. We should have lunch."

I looked out the window and waved, to be polite, but didn't give her an answer. She threw in the lunch part to sound affable, but I knew she didn't mean it. We never ate together or talked outside of school functions.

When I got to the gallery, Stella was busy on the phone at her desk. She raised her hand at me and pointed to the back room. Kate and Liam were already here.

"Good morning," I said when I opened the door.

Liam stood up from the stool, green eyes gleaming, dimples piercing. "Abby, I'm excited to start. Kate was showing me the list of clients, and she gave me my first assignment."

Kate and I had moved furniture around and made room for one more easel for Liam.

"That's great. I'm not going to repeat everything Kate said, so if you need anything or if you have any questions, please don't hesitate to ask."

"Of course." Liam smiled and sat back on his stool.

"Oh, there is one more thing." Kate handed him a swath of folded black canvas.

When he held it out in front of him, he let out a small chuckle. "I love it. I've never worn one of these before."

The front of the apron read: *Messier the apron, the greater the artist.*

While Kate and Liam got to work, I went to the computer to the list of customers. After I studied the description of the next in line order, I grabbed a new, primed canvas.

I gathered the different-sized brushes, picked up my palette and oil paints, and lost myself in color, lines, and the heady fumes of paints and thinners. When I was deep in my world of clouds, ocean, and palm trees, I lived inside the painting. My toes dug into the soft, velvety sand, and cool water washed over my feet. The palm trees with coconuts dangling overhead gave me shelter and shade as I watched the boats sail past, wishing I was there with my family. Time was irrelevant in this magical world.

"Abby. You've got a delivery." Stella's happy voice rang through the speaker.

I was startled, my paintbrush flying out of my hand. With a hand over my pounding heart, I pressed the button on the landline phone. What time was it? Almost noon.

"Maybe lower the volume?" Kate snorted.

Liam shrugged and gave a cute boyish grin. Something must be up. Stella sounded too bubbly.

"I'll be back," I said, and went out the door. "Stella? You have something for me?"

Her smile was brighter than the afternoon sun. "So, what happened this weekend with Ian?"

I narrowed my eyes. "What do you mean? I already told you. We went zip-lining."

"Uh-huh." She gave me a suspicious look.

I wagged a finger at her. "Nope. Don't say that. Something happens when you say that. So, what delivery is so important you pulled me out of work?"

"It's over there." She gestured with a tilt of her head.

I searched for a box from UPS or FedEx. If it were an envelope, she would have handed it to me. I half-turned to ask her where it was, but then I saw a glass vase filled with flowers—birds of paradise, gerbera daisies, chamomile, orchids, and lilies—the most elegant, beautiful arrangement I had ever seen.

"Who sent it?" I asked, stunned. "Are you sure it's for me?"

"Go take a look. It has your name on the card. But I will gladly read it for you."

I hiked up my eyebrows. "How do I know you didn't already read it?"

"Because it's sealed." She gave me those innocent puppy eyes.

I shook my head and smiled. "You're lucky I love you so much." I inhaled the sweet flowery scent and picked up the note with a shaky hand.

"You mean you need me too much." She cracked up. "Without me, you have no idea what to do with the invoices, the website, and now how to pay Liam."

I shot her a pointed look and rolled my eyes playfully, then I opened the note. As I read it, I felt the weight of Stella's stare and fought hard to suppress the smile creeping on my lips.

> Dearest Abby,
> A reminder that I'm proud of you for being
> brave. Not everyone has the courage to do

something they fear. This Saturday is my turn.
You might have to hold my hand.
Best,
Ian

I reread the note. A swarm of butterflies fluttered pleasantly in my stomach. Then something rested on my shoulder. I realized it was Stella's chin when she said, "Awww. That is the cutest love letter I've ever seen."

I jerked. "Stella. When did you ..."

Stella took a step back, her lips pinched together, her eyes dancing as she feigned innocence.

"It's not a love letter." I shoved the note inside my back pocket. "Ian is a friend, that's all. I can have male friends, right?" I didn't mean to sound rude.

Stella raised both hands and walked backward to her desk. "Of course, you can."

This friendliness between Stella and me was my fault. I had come to treat her more like a sister, over the years, than an employee. The close bond was inevitable, especially because Stella was kind and loving, even when she was cracking jokes.

"Sorry. I didn't mean—"

She sat on her chair and faced the computer screen. "No, no, no. It's my fault. I just want the best for you."

The backroom door banged open, and Kate came rushing out.

"What happened?" She glanced between Stella and me, and her eyes popped open wide when they found the bouquet of flowers. "From?"

"Ian." I gave my sister a don't-you-dare-read-more-into-this look. "He's trying to apologize for making me go zip-lining." Sort of the truth. Even though he hadn't written those words, that was the intention.

"Oh." Kate's voice squeaked.

"If you two don't mind, I'm going to leave the flowers on the table. It brightens up the space."

"Sure," Kate said.

"Your flowers. Your gallery. You do whatever you want." Stella gave me a tight-lipped smile and turned away.

Stella could be prickly, but she forgave easily. When the room went eerily quiet and the tension thickened, I had to lighten the mood.

"How was your weekend, Stella?"

Stella slowly peered up and smirked. "It was perfect." Her face beamed sunshine and rainbows. "He took me to an upscale restaurant, then we went for a drink, and then we made out. But we stopped there, you know, because that's my first date rule."

One thing about Stella—she held nothing back and always said what she was thinking.

"Oh," I said. "So you two are …"

Stella crossed her arms on the desk. "We're taking it slow. I don't want to rush into anything, and neither does he. So, first zip-lining and now horseback riding. You wild thing. What has become of you?"

"I know, right?" I snorted. "I'm such a party girl."

Kate stayed behind to chat with Stella while I went back to work. I'd thought Liam would ask questions, but he kept to himself and focused on the painting in front of him. Just before I picked up a paintbrush, I texted Ian.

> Abby: Thank you for the beautiful flowers.
> You didn't have to do that.

I was going to put the phone down, but a text pinged.

> Ian: I had to do something to bribe you to
> hold my hand during horseback riding.

I smiled and swiped my fingers fast over the letters.

> Abby: No need to bribe. That's what
> friends do.

> Ian: Then Lee is a terrible friend. He won't
> hold my hand.

A small snicker squeaked out of me, and Liam turned to look. I sent a laughing emoji, and he sent me a heart one back.

I stared at the red beating heart a bit longer than necessary.

Chapter Twenty~Three — Horseback Riding

T he remaining week went by in a flash with roughly the same routine every day. Take Tyler to school. Go to work. Come home. Today would be different. Tyler woke up early, so I didn't go for my run.

"When is Ian coming?" Tyler asked, sitting on the sofa and looking out the window.

"Very soon, sweetheart. He said he was on his way." I wiped a wet dish with a towel and placed it inside the cabinet.

Outside, a car door slammed, and Tyler jumped up. His footsteps pounded across the floor, and the door creaked open. I grabbed a backpack, did a quick glance around the house to make sure all the windows were closed, and walked out. Tyler was already in the back seat.

Ian gave me a peck on the cheek and opened the door for me. As he backed out of the driveway, he asked Tyler about school and his friends.

"I'm glad you like school." Ian looked in the rearview mirror at my son. "You know, Lee was my best friend when we were your age."

"I know," Tyler said matter-of-factly. "Lee told me. He told me some funny stories."

I craned my neck to get a better look at my son. His lips were parted from laughing, and he looked so happy. Seeing him like this reassured me I was doing okay as his mother. God knows I tried my best, but happiness is hard to deliver.

"Anything new at school, Ty?" Ian asked. "Girlfriend I should know about?"

"No." Tyler laughed nervously.

I wasn't sure if that was truly a no, or if he was too shy to admit it.

"Well ..." Tyler crossed his arms. "Something is happening at school next month, but I can't go."

I stiffened, anticipating what was coming next. I should have told Tyler not to say anything.

"Why not?" Ian met my gaze momentarily, concern flashing in those gorgeous eyes.

"It's father and son miniature golf night, and I don't have a dad." His voice lowered to a mumble as he stared at his shoes.

I'd thought we had gone past this, that he understood, but clearly, it still troubled him. Maybe kids at school had said something. I wanted to cut in and change the subject, but what could I say? The words were already spoken.

Ian frowned and raked his fingers through his hair. His other hand tightened on the wheel. I parted my lips to say something, but I didn't know what. My heart broke for Tyler, who waited expectantly, and I hated how awkward the situation was for Ian. I'd never want him to volunteer out of obligation.

I thought about saying, *Tyler and I already had this talk, and he's fine.* Or *This isn't your problem, so don't worry about it.* But the words wouldn't come.

Ian signaled left and turned. "Why don't you ask if you can bring an uncle? I'll go with you. It'll be fun. That's if you would want to go with me."

"Shiver me timbers. You would?" Tyler's voice boomed in the small space. "Did you hear that, Mom? Ian wants to take me."

"I-I—" I couldn't finish.

Ian raised his eyebrows in an open how-about-it smile. He seemed to genuinely want to go. He could have said he was busy. He hadn't had to offer. But this felt wrong. Not fair to Ian or my son. And if I could be honest with myself, seeing Ian and Tyler together would spread gossip through the community. The town wasn't that large when you discounted tourists, and that could open Ian and me up to unwanted questions.

I wouldn't be embarrassed to be with Ian—if we *were* a couple. But I didn't want people to have the wrong idea at Tyler's school. Not that I cared what others thought, anyway.

Ian grabbed my hand, but his eyes stayed on the road. "I don't mind taking Tyler. I promise I won't take him to the bar after. I'll bring him straight home."

I let out a puff of air, a laugh of a sort.

"If you don't trust me with your son, then—"

"That's not it. I just don't want to trouble you."

"I wouldn't have said anything if I didn't want to do it. Besides, what are friends for? Tyler and I are going to beat everyone, right, Ty? We're going to rule at miniature golf."

Tyler, who had been quiet and listening intently to the conversation, blurted, "Awesome. Cool. Thank you, Ian." Then he looked out the window, and my heart melted at the sight of his broad smile.

I tried to take back my hand, but Ian held on a little longer, like he didn't want to let go. He squeezed it once, then released me to turn the wheel.

When we arrived at Silver Falls, Lee, Kate, and Bridget were already there. Cassie, our instructor, came out to greet us. She was young and cute, and her eyes frequently turned toward Ian.

I tried to pay, but Ian said it was his turn, since Lee had paid for the zip-lining. Lee paying for Kate was fine by me, but they had to stop treating me. I would have to return the favor next time.

After we put on our helmets, I adjusted my backpack. Kate took out her mega-camera and insisted we take pictures. We took single and group pictures while Cassie brought out the beautiful horses—four bigger ones and two smaller ones.

"This is mine, right?" Ian pointed to the small black horse. "Because I'm not getting on that beast. They're all looking at me like they want to eat me."

We all laughed.

"You're silly." Bridget's smile grew bigger, showing off all of her teeth, one missing at the bottom.

"Don't worry," Cassie said to Ian, and winked. "I'll take good care of you."

I bet you will.

I shook off my thoughts. It was all innocent, but that wink— jealousy spiked through me, surprising myself. I had no right. Ian could date whomever he wanted.

Ian's lips tugged, but I couldn't read his expression with his dark sunglasses on. Though I wondered what he thought of her. She was beautiful, fit, and tanned. Between the flirting and the staring, she'd left no doubt as to her interest.

"Besides," Cassie added, "we're going slow for the kiddos, and this is the easiest trail we have to offer."

After Cassie helped us climb up on our horses, she demonstrated how to steer the reins. We filed in one line behind Cassie, the horses' hooves clopping along the paved path. The roads became straight and smooth like the sky above. My backpack bounced on my back, where sweat already gathered between my shoulder blades.

After a short ride, our horses plodded onto a packed dirt road. Dust puffed from under the horses' hooves and hung in the air behind us. The breeze caressed my cheeks and rustled the palm tree leaves in quiet applause as we passed. Tropical foliage in every shade of green lined the trail.

Ian's horse came up beside mine, and I looked over in surprise.

"You doing okay?" I asked.

Cassie had instructed us to stay in a single-file line. Ian had told me he felt nervous about riding a horse. However, he hid the fear well.

"This is nice," Ian said. "Taking it slow and easy. It's not as bad as I thought it would be. I might say otherwise if we were riding faster. It's a good thing I could use the kids as an excuse for taking the easy route."

I nodded. "To be honest, I don't like riding fast, either. I feel like I'm losing control, and perhaps the horse might decide to kick me off."

"Well, don't get yourself kicked off the horse. I won't be able to catch you this time."

"You know what they say, third time is a charm. And I expect you to jump off the horse like the knight in shining armor you are and catch my fall."

"Okay, it's a deal. What Abby wants, Abby gets."

Silence crept in for a short time until I spoke. "So, now you can check horse backing riding off your bucket list."

"True, but I bet my mother is frowning down at me and giving that *mom* glare."

"No, she's not." I laughed. "You can prove to her that you're just fine."

"I feel like I'm cheating, though."

"What do you mean?" I sneaked a peek to the front, wondering when Cassie would look behind her and catch Ian.

"Well, zip-lining was obviously more terrifying than riding a horse on this kiddy trail."

"I sure hope your bucket list isn't all about doing dangerous things." I sounded playfully appalled.

Ian chuckled and scrubbed the side of his temple, as if contemplating. "Well, let's see. Skydiving. Swimming with the sharks. Mountain climbing. Water rafting. Bungee—"

I furrowed my brow. "Okay, I get the picture. But there are things not as dangerous, right?"

He looked thoughtful. "I can't remember."

"Then let horseback riding be on the safe list, and you can cross it off."

"Sounds good to me," he sang. He ducked his head toward me and lowered his voice. "You ready for tomorrow night?"

A few days ago, Lee had let me know that the day after horseback riding, he planned to propose to Kate. He had asked Ian and me to help. We had to get things set ahead of time, and I had to bring Kate to Ian's house. I had asked Kate to have dinner with Tyler and me, so we were set.

Lee wanted to propose to Kate at the beach just as the sun set, then he planned to take her to Italy in the summer. His parents would be there, as well. On their way home, Lee and Kate would stop by Los Angeles and visit my parents.

"Look." Ian gestured toward the front of the line. "Kate is taking pictures of us."

I acted on reflexes, leaning into him without thought, and smiled.

"That camera is like her third arm." Ian chuckled. "Doesn't she get tired?"

A strand of hair fell over my nose as a quick breeze passed by. I pushed it behind my ear. "Actually, she saves me the trouble so I don't have to do it."

"Straight line, please," Cassie's voice boomed in the air.

"Uh oh, I better get back to my spot before the sergeant shows her devil horns."

I laughed, and Ian slowed. The dirt road became grassy, then we meandered downward along a winding route. When we reached the bottom, we got off our horses and tied their reins to a wooden post.

We went on foot from there. Ian offered to hold my backpack, and I handed it to him. We pushed through the tall grass, and Cassie led the way down the steep, rocky path.

"Hold on to your children and the rope, please," Cassie hollered.

I was about to hold Tyler's hand, but Ian rushed ahead and beat me to it.

"Let me help, Abby." Ian glanced over his shoulder at me. "If he falls, he'll bring you down with him." He was right, and I wasn't going to argue with him. "Put one hand on the rope and one hand on my shoulder. I'll help you down, too."

Ian's muscular shoulder was difficult to grasp, so I balled the back of his T-shirt to make a fist. The soft splash of the waterfall filled my ears, and mist dampened my face. Once we passed the slippery path, we were at the hidden waterfall.

"Wow, look at that." Tyler pointed to the waterfall, its bottom pooling into a stream.

The stream led to another drop. We were in the middle of a two-tiered waterfall. I inhaled deep, fresh air as I glanced about. Nothing but trees and shrubs surrounded us.

"You're welcome to take pictures and swim," Cassie said. "We can stay for half an hour before another tour comes by."

After everyone drank water from Kate's backpack underneath a tree, Bridget and Tyler took off their shoes and waded at the shallow end. Ian and Lee stood by the kids while Kate took pictures.

"Are you having fun?" Kate asked, pressed against the camera's viewfinder.

"I'm with you. We have fun no matter what we do."

Kate shifted from side to side and kicked loose a few pebbles. She moved forward and backward, trying to get the best angle.

"We're still on for tomorrow, right?" my sister asked.

"Yes, we are. Unless you need to cancel."

She hadn't looked at me yet, and that was a good thing. I was a terrible liar, and my cheeks felt hot. Ian, Lee, and the kids threw pebbles to see who could throw the farthest.

Kate lowered her camera. "No. I'm good. Lee is busy with work. And Bridget is going to a birthday party. Is Tyler going, too?"

"No. He wasn't invited. I think it's just the girls." I glanced over at Ian and Tyler, who gave each other high fives.

Kate scrunched her eyebrows to the center. "Oh." She sounded surprised—reasonable, since they were in the same classroom and kids usually invited the whole class. "Okay, then. It'll be the three of us."

It was a flimsy excuse, but I'd needed something.

"Sounds good." I leaned my back against the tree. "What time do you plan on dropping by? I might go to the gallery for a bit."

Kate pointed the camera at the waterfall and clicked. "What time would you like for me to come?"

Lee had asked me to bring Kate to Ian's house by seven, but she should fix herself up and wear something more elegant than jeans and a T-shirt.

"I'm going to take the three of us out somewhere nice, so you need to dress up. They have a dress code."

Kate crossed her arms. I was sure she could see right through me.

"What's the occasion?" She peered up to the clouds, then angled her head. "Am I forgetting something?"

"No. Nothing like that." I flashed a glance toward Lee, Ian, Tyler, and Bridget, splashing water at each other and laughing. "Can't I just take my sister to a nice restaurant?"

"Fine, then I get to treat you next time." She picked up her camera to take pictures.

"Who said I was paying for tomorrow's dinner in the first place? I planned to make you pay," I teased, edging closer to the water.

"I knew it!" She grinned and kicked water at me.

I backed away. "Hey ..." I stopped when I saw Cassie talking to Ian.

She hooked strands of hair over her ear and leaned closer to him, her shoulder almost touching his. The waterfall made it impossible for me to hear them, but they were laughing. When Cassie placed a hand on Ian's arm, I frowned.

Kate raised an eyebrow. I ignored her and shifted my gaze to Tyler. But, damn it. Every other second, my eyes slid over to Ian and Cassie.

They must be exchanging phone numbers, because they both had their cell phones out. None of my business. Ian and I were friends, nothing more. I was the one who'd made that clear.

My sister poked my shoulder and whispered, "If you don't snatch him soon, he's going to get caught by someone else."

I wanted to tell her that was fine, but Kate rushed to Lee and Bridget to take more photos. I went to Tyler, who was checking out the pebbles under the water. I heard the sound of splashing behind me and felt Ian's presence. My heart thudded too fast.

"Look, Abby." He pointed to the sky, his warm breath against my face. "It's a rainbow."

"Rainbow!" Bridget squealed.

When Kate and I were little, we made a wish every time we saw a rainbow. Seeing a rainbow after a storm meant that good things would come our way. It sure would for Kate, tomorrow. She would be engaged to the love of her life, and I couldn't be happier for her.

"Make a wish," Ian said.

I turned and met Ian's gaze. His warm smile and the twinkle in his eyes made me forget the world, made me think wishes did come true. But he could not grant my wish.

Chapter Twenty~Four — Engagement

I dropped off Tyler at his friend's house for a play date the next day, then Ian picked me up. This was the first time I had been in the car alone with him. I shifted in my seat. Looked out the window. Scrolled through my phone. My palms even started to sweat.

Ian turned into the main road. "Do we need to buy tickets for the miniature golfing event? It's my first time." He flashed a dorky grin.

I smiled and shook my head.

"Don't worry about it. I already got your tickets." I hadn't yet, but he didn't need to know. "But thank you for thinking about it. I really appreciate this. It's not too late to back out."

"I said I would take him, and it's not a big deal. Besides, one day I'll have kids of my own, and it'll be good practice."

You're going to make a great husband and father someday. The family will be lucky to have you.

"Well, you can practice with us all you want," I said, and immediately regretted opening my mouth, but the words came easily. *Oh, God.* I sucked at this friendship thing. I changed the topic to cover up my mistake. "I can't believe Lee is going to be my brother-in-law."

Ian changed lanes and said, "He's been more than ready. I think, if he could, he would have proposed to Kate when they first met." He let out a short laugh. "Lee had his share of unsuccessful relationships, then he found Kate. You know when someone is the one for you. You feel an undeniable connection, and you can't let it go. I'm getting all mushy, aren't I?"

"No, not at all." I patted his arm. *Don't touch him.* Every time I did, something fluttered inside me. "So, how about you? Anyone special?"

I already knew the answer, but I didn't want to assume. Since we were on the topic of relationships, I figured this was a question a friend could ask another friend.

Ian raked a hand through his hair and glanced at me before setting his eyes on the road. "You won't judge me, right? I want to be honest with you."

"Your past is your past. We all have dated someone we're not proud of." That seemed like the right thing to say, though I was thinking more of people I knew than myself. I had always been the perfect daughter. Perfect girlfriend. Boring. Never taking a risk type of girl.

Ian released a long sigh. "I've dated, but only a couple were more than a casual hookup. The relationships didn't last long. Lee said I've been dating women I don't want to fall in love with because I wasn't ready for a serious commitment. Maybe he was right."

"Maybe you'll want to settle down when you meet the right person," I said.

I glanced out the window. The view had changed from grassy land to the ocean, and serenity filled my core. I kept my eyes rooted there.

We fell into a comfortable silence as we drove along the coast and listened to the radio. We talked about our high school and college years, and before I knew it, he had parked in his garage.

He asked me to direct the decorators, and he would help the caterer. We had plenty of time, but the excitement had my adrenaline pumping, and I wanted everything to be just right.

Ian and I were a perfect team as we spent the next hour creating an enchanting scene. When everything was done, I stepped back to marvel at the view. Electric candles in tall glass vases lined the backyard to the giant white gazebo on the beach. Inside was a table set for two with rose petals scattered about on the mat.

On the table were trays with dome-shaped silver lids that kept the food warm and a pretty display of candle arrangements and flowers. A wine bottle inside an ice bucket with two elegant glasses was at the table to the back. And inside a bakery glass display was a cake that read: *Will You Marry Me?*

Tears filled my eyes. What a beautiful setting, and what a gorgeous view. By the time Ian and I had finished, the sun had set lower, tinting the sky with periwinkle. The water sparkled with sunlight diamonds. I could stare at this view all day.

"Looks like we're all set." Ian's voice came from behind me.

I stiffened when he put his arms around my shoulders. The smell of mint and ocean breeze enveloped me.

"It's going to be the perfect marriage proposal." I craned my neck to face him.

"Almost. It'll be second to mine."

He sounded sure of himself. But his confidence drew me to him, besides his charming personality, good looks, and how great he was with children.

He blinked those long eyelashes, his eyes turning molten gold under the sunlight. His face seemed to glow as his lips spread into an irresistible smirk, his gaze bored into mine with longing. He looked absolutely heavenly.

Wind whisked my hair across my eyes. Ian pushed back the strands over my ear and lowered his finger down my cheek, down my neck, and over my shoulder. I shuddered. My pulse raced. I was lost in that moment, lost to him.

When Ian's gaze lowered to my lips, I swallowed nervously, wondering if I had imagined him edging closer to me. I thought I might want this kiss, had actually even dreamed about it a couple of times, but I would wake up feeling guilty. If I let him, would it hurt our friendship?

Steve. Tyler. Guilt socked me in the gut.

I gradually lowered my gaze to the soft sand between my toes and spewed out words. "I should get going. I have to meet my sister back at my house to bring her here on time. She can't be late. And I need to pick up Tyler."

I tugged Ian's shirt to break whatever was happening between us because it couldn't happen. Any more temptation, and I might give in and let him kiss me. God knows I wanted to, at least in my dreams. I wasn't ready, and this amazing man deserved someone who would give him all their heart and soul.

Kate arrived at my house at six-thirty on the dot. She wore a spaghetti-strapped black dress that hugged her curves. Her long soft curls bounced, and her light makeup accentuated her features, bringing out her eyes, her cheekbones, and those lips. She looked absolutely stunning.

Tyler came out from his bedroom. "Hi, Auntie Kate."

"Wow, Ty. Look at you. You look so handsome." Kate kissed his forehead. "Are you going to be our date tonight?"

Tyler was dressed in dark pants and a long-sleeve top. He had sleeked his hair back without my help. My mother's heart swelled, proud of him and saddened by it at the same time. He was growing up too fast. Time needed to slow down.

He raised his chin. "I sure am."

"Well then." I grabbed my purse. "We better get going, or we're going to be late."

After we got into my car, Kate said, "You still haven't told me where we're going."

I shrugged and gave her a sly smile. "You'll see."

Kate looked over to Tyler in the back seat. "Do you know where we're going? Your mother is being very secretive."

I looked in the rearview mirror at my son, grinning. "I don't know, Auntie Kate. I only care about eating yummy food."

Kate and I laughed, then she gazed out the window.

When the roads became familiar, she slapped my arm lightly. "Are we having dinner at Ian's house? Is this the surprise?"

"You'll see." My expression remained neutral as I parked in the driveaway. It was so difficult to contain my excitement. I wanted to tell her everything. "Tyler, stay in the car. I'll be right back. Kate, come with me. I need your help."

I didn't give my son a chance to respond. He had no idea what was going on. I got out of the car in a hurry and walked with Kate, who was looking at me suspiciously.

"What's going on with you?" she asked when we got to the front door.

I rang the doorbell and inhaled and exhaled. My sister was the one getting proposed to, and I was freaking out, my nerves all over the place.

The door opened, and Ian appeared. My breath caught in my throat as his eyes pinned on me, then his gaze lowered, taking in all of me in the white linen dress.

That was when I realized I wasn't nervous for my sister, but for myself. Coming back to his house where the almost-kiss had happened had me tangled in knots.

Ian wore dark pants and a white linen button-up, sleeves rolled up a quarter of the way. The white on his tanned skin gave him a crisp but relaxed Mediterranean vibe. I couldn't deny he looked good. Too good. We almost looked like a couple who coordinated their outfits.

"Kate, Abby. Come in."

"Do you know what's going on, Ian?" Kate said. "Abby is acting strange."

"Kate." I gripped her shoulder, forcing her to look at me. "I'll explain everything tomorrow, but someone special is waiting for you outside. Go. Right now. Hurry." I lightly shoved her to get her going.

She knew I was talking about Lee. As she looked over her shoulder at me, she quickened her step, her smile grew wider, and her eyes sparkled as bright as the ocean gleaming under the sunlight.

I turned back to Ian. I was going to ask if he wanted to join Tyler and me for dinner, but I stopped when his eyebrows furrowed. Something between us felt off.

"Abby." He sounded uncertain. "I didn't know you were ... I thought ..."

"We should get going. Looks like Lee's girl is here," a female voice said from the kitchen. A gorgeous brunette strutted into the family room. When her eyes met mine, she beamed a smile.

Ian glanced between us. A heavy tension seeped in the air, and he went rigid. "Abby, this is Jackie."

"I'm Kate's sister." I shook her hand.

"Oh ..." She smiled again, beautiful and bright. "I see the resemblance. Will you be staying? Because Ian and I are leaving." Her voice was pleasant enough, but ...

Wench. Walk the plank.

Hurt flickered inside me, and I tried to stuff it down. Ian and I were friends, and he could date whomever he wanted, as I'd told myself when the horseback riding guide had been flirting with him. But he'd hidden his dating life well, whether intentionally or not.

Ian frowned, but he didn't say anything. What could he say? She had merely asked a question and stated a fact.

"I'm not staying," I said. "My part was to drop off my sister. Well, have a good time." I didn't bother to look at Ian or say goodbye to him. There was no need.

A hand grabbed my shoulder. "Abby, wait. I'll walk you out."

I turned to Ian. "That's okay. I have somewhere to be, and you need to get going."

Ian ignored my request and walked me to the door. "You look very nice. Where are you going?"

"You have your date, and I have mine. Have a good evening, Ian." Before he could say another word, I shut the door behind me.

I shook my head, chastising myself for acting like a scorned woman, as if he'd done something wrong. Where was this jealousy coming from? I didn't like it one bit. I desperately wanted to see if Ian had come out, but instead, I hopped in the car.

"Mom? What's going on?"

"Sorry, Ty. I'll explain everything during dinner." I turned on the engine and backed away. I wanted to get the hell out of there.

"Mom. Look. There's Ian." Tyler glued his face to the window.

"Can we ask him to come to dinner with us?"

Ian was alone, standing there watching me drive off. He looked conflicted or mad. I wasn't sure. It didn't matter. He had a date, and he should be with her.

"No, Ty." I softened my tone. "He's busy. He already has plans."

It was better this way. Tyler was getting too attached to Ian, and perhaps, if I were being honest, so was I.

Later that night, Kate called me on her way home with Lee and sent me a photo of her hand with the ring. They got on the speakerphone and thanked me for my help. They had also called Mom and Dad to let them know the engagement was final, even though they had known ahead of time. Then Kate gave me the amazing details of their dinner and how Lee had proposed to her.

After we hung up, I cried silently in bed. Happy tears for my sister. Excited she had asked me to be her maid of honor. Sad tears of missing Steve and frustrated sobs for the conflicted feelings that were growing for Ian.

Chapter Twenty~Five — After

When I walked into work on Monday morning, Liam and Kate were leaning over Stella's desk, admiring Kate's ring. She had shared the details of Lee's proposal with them.

"That is one giant rock." Stella's eyes were glued to the diamond while she held Kate's hand. "How big is it?"

"I'm guessing it's like five carats?" Liam said and shrugged when we stared at him. "What? My brother owns a jewelry store."

"When's the wedding?" Stella asked.

"We haven't decided yet, but I'll let you know as soon as we set the date." Kate brought her hand to the sunlight filtering in from the front window. The diamond sparkled right in my eyes.

"Hey, put that down before you blind me." I snorted. "Kauai has good weather all year round, so you might want to check quickly. Dates will be taken fast, not just from locals. Couples come from all over the world to get married here."

"Good idea, sis. That's why you're my maid of honor, and Ian is Lee's best man."

"Awwww. That's so sweet," Stella said genuinely, with no hint of sarcasm this time.

"Well, congratulations, Kate." Liam clasped his hands. "You ladies enjoy your talk about weddings and stuff. I need to get back to work."

"I'll be right behind you," I said, and focused back on my sister. "Ian is Lee's best man?"

Of course, he was.

"Are you okay?" Kate rested her hand on my back. "You look baffled or mad."

Stella looked away from the computer and swirled her rolling chair to face us. "Abby made that face after you mentioned Ian's name. I think she's confused about her feelings."

"What? Am not." But I was.

I went to the table, grabbed a paper mug, and poured myself a coffee. I already had a cup at home, but I needed a second one. I had tossed and turned the night before with another dream of Steve and Ian.

The dreams were short, and my memory of them had faded. I only remembered waking up hot and bothered and unsure if I'd been kissing Ian or Steve.

Stella furrowed her brow. "Uh-huh. You keep telling yourself that and someone is going to get hurt. You better make a move soon, or someone else will. Isaac told me single women from their circle of rich friends"—she used her index and middle finger to make air quotes—"have been knocking down Ian's door ever since they found out he's back."

"Ian and I are just friends." I tried to sound convincing, but how was Stella supposed to believe me if I couldn't convince myself?

I took a sip of the coffee and spat it out. "Crap." I wiped my mouth with a napkin I grabbed off the table.

"Are you okay?" Kate rushed over to me.

"I forgot I was drinking something hot." I fanned my open mouth and stopped when I realized how ridiculous I was acting.

"See." Stella bobbed her shoulder. "She gets distracted when I mention Ian."

"I do not," I said, sounding like a child. "Maybe I shouldn't go to the auction."

"What? Why?" Kate crossed her arms, leaning to one side of her hip. "Those tickets are expensive, and Ian bought one for you."

I inhaled a long breath and exhaled a longer one as I peered up to the ceiling. "It won't be a loss for him. He can take someone else. I think he's dating someone named Jackie. I met her when I dropped you off at Ian's house yesterday."

Kate raised her eyebrows. "So that's what's going on."

I took another sip, not liking Kate and Stella scrutinizing me like I was in the wrong.

"You two are acting strange." I frowned.

"Oh, I get it now." Stella nodded, her eyes sparkled in amusement. I hated when they talked like they were in on a secret.

"Anyway," Kate said. "You should go. If you don't go, then it'll seem like you're ignoring him on purpose. Besides, Ian isn't picking you up, right? My understanding is that he's meeting us there."

I lifted my lips to the side. "I guess you're right. Fine. I'll go."

"Also, Abby ..." Stella pointed up a finger. "Remember, one of your paintings is up for auction. It's good PR."

"I suppose." I sighed defeatedly.

Kate would be with Lee and Stella with Isaac. I would end up being the fifth wheel. And I didn't like going to functions where I was forced to make small talk.

"You'll be fine," Stella stressed. "You have us."

"Thank you," I said. "I love you both very much."

As usual, Stella liked to put her own twist on things when our topic became serious.

"No sweat. I have to be nice to you. You pay me." She snorted. "Oh, wait. *I* do." She cackled. "It's a good thing I'm trustworthy, or else you would never know if I was stealing from you."

Stella was joking, but Kate and I exchanged a wary glance. Not because we didn't trust Stella, but at the alarming thought of something happening to her. Kate and I ought to know how to manage the accounts, too. I put that in my mental notes.

Steve had been the one who had overseen our family finances. He'd shown me how to pay the bills, where our stocks and mutual bonds were located, not that we had much. We had been starting to save. Had he passed away suddenly, I would've been in a bind.

I tossed my empty paper cup into the trash and leveled my eyes at my sister. "Did you tell Bridget she gets to be the flower girl?"

Kate stopped arranging the tea bags and the wooden sticks. "I did. She's too excited. She's already practicing walking straight and pretending to scatter rose petals."

"How cute," Stella cooed. "And Tyler will be the ring bearer, I assume?"

I shrugged, lowering my head as if my feelings were hurt. "I have no idea. No one has asked."

Kate lightly smacked my arm. "Of course, Tyler will be the ring bearer. We haven't even set the date yet. Then we'll talk."

"Fine. I forgive you. Anyway, enough talking. We have deadlines to meet."

The wind chimes tinkled a soft, beautiful melody, and customers walked in. While I went to the backroom, Kate greeted the couple.

Chapter Twenty~Six — Charity

The drive to Romanos' place was up a hill and curvy, but the expanded view of the ocean took my breath away. To the left of the ocean were the big hotels, and all the way to my right were beautiful homes with the same view.

"How do you know the Romano family?" I asked Lee.

Lee's bright eyes reflected in the rearview mirror. "Their family and mine go way back."

I should have known. Lee knew everyone with large pockets.

The curvy road straightened, and the palm trees lining either side, like the tunnel tree, led the way to a security booth.

Lee gave the man inside the booth our names, then the gate slid open. I had imagined what the mansion would look like, but this place was bigger than Lee's. It looked more like a castle with a private street and entry.

Five luxury vehicles were in front of us, waiting for the valet. When we got out of the car, we hiked up several steps to the massive glass front door. Security guards with guns were stationed inside and outside by the doors. Several men dressed in dark suits greeted us, checked off our names on his tablet, then let us in.

An elegant brass chandelier dangled from the high ceiling. Staircases curved upward to the second floor. A check-in table where women dropped off sweaters or purses was stationed to the right.

I was glad I had decided on a long black satin dress with a high slit up to my thigh, or I might have looked underdressed. All the women wore expensive ballgowns and had sparkling jewelry adorning their necks, ears, and fingers.

I followed Kate, admiring how her strapless black gown hugged her curves and swished around her ankles. She was gorgeous. And Lee, walking beside her, was clad in a dark tailored suit, looking classy. A million-dollar couple.

We gathered inside a large room. Guests mingled and clumped in small groups. Some held flutes of champagne, and others held martini glasses. An older woman dressed in a red gown, with honey brown hair, came up to us.

"Lee, how have you been, darling?" she said.

When she kissed his cheeks from left to right, I'd caught sight of her large diamond ring on her left hand.

"I just got engaged," Lee said. "This is my fiancée Kate and her sister, Abby."

The woman kissed the air beside Kate's face, and then mine. "Oh, how lovely they are," she said to Lee. Then her eyes went to my sister's ring. "Beautiful. Well, congratulations. I see Ian by the stage. I have a few questions for him. See you at the auction. Just don't bet against me." She winked at Lee and strutted away.

I glanced in the direction she was headed, but didn't see Ian. I wondered if he'd brought a date. Jackie, perhaps? Or maybe someone new.

Stop thinking about who or how many women he's dating. It's none of your business.

Farther inside, more guests stopped us to say hello. Lee introduced them to Kate and me, but they mostly spoke to Lee. A waiter holding a silver tray with champagne flutes came up to us. Kate took two and handed one to Lee, and I took one.

I savored the cool liquid as I people watched, trying not to appear awkward or fidget, all the while wondering what was I doing here. I drank more sips to have something to do with my hands and listened to the instrumental music.

Stella and Isaac waved at me from a distance, then got busy talking to a group of people I assumed were Isaac's friends. Stella seemed comfortable, laughing at whatever they were saying. She fit right in, unlike me.

Other waiters came by in the classic catering uniform—black pants and white button-up shirts, holding silver trays with appetizers: some offered seafood, crackers and cheese, and finger sandwiches.

"Lee, did you bring two beautiful dates? Couldn't decide?" A nice-looking man shook Lee's hand. He was as tall as Lee with broad shoulders, tanned skin, and beautiful brown eyes. Lee chuckled. He introduced Kate to Kyle as his fiancée and me as his soon-to-be sister-in-law.

"So nice to meet you, Abby." Kyle kissed the back of my hand. "If you need company, come find me. I'll take good care of you." He winked.

"Not going to happen," Lee said playfully. "Ian."

"Oh, I see. Well, I don't see a ring on her finger." He let out a chuckle. "Find me later, Abby, or I'll find you. I hate to have to run, but I'm supposed to be helping."

I thought it was strange that Lee had mentioned Ian's name. I hadn't come as Ian's date.

"We should find our seats," Lee said and guided us outside to the backyard.

What a view. Palm trees, hibiscus, and plumerias lined the path to a large water fountain that shot out to a grand decorative pool. I passed by a giant white tent and a stage.

"Abby. Kate. Lee." A perky voice called from behind, followed by tapping heels.

I whirled to see Jessica Conner in her lowcut black ballgown with rhinestones beaded on the top. Her dress was straight and tight, even to the bottom, so that she waddled like an excited penguin toward us.

Jessica seemed taller, for some reason. I peered down at her shoes. Oh, her three-inch heels … as if she needed the extra height.

Be nice, Abby.

"I didn't know you three were coming." Breathless, Jessica spoke like we were good friends. She glanced between the three of us. Her eyes grew rounder when my sister wiggled her fingers in front of her.

I bet Kate couldn't wait to show off her ring. Many of the single women in Kauai had been after Lee at one point or another, including Jessica.

"When did that happen?" Jessica sounded surprised.

Kate coiled her arm around Lee's. "Yesterday."

"Congratulations." She sounded genuine. "That's a gorgeous ring. Well, the news will spread. So get ready. Anyway, I need to get back to my date."

My sister and I exchanged an eyeroll, then continued ahead with Lee. A gentleman blocked us, holding a tablet. Behind him, white chairs lined the neatly cut lawn, row after row. He escorted us to the middle of the first row, even though I had expected to be sitting toward the back empty seats.

Each chair held a pamphlet and something that looked like a fan. Oh, of course, a bidding stick.

I settled in my seat and smiled at the person to the right of me. I wondered who would be sitting in the empty seat between us. Ian? As I waited, I flipped through the pamphlet. The donation items were listed and the person or the company who had donated them.

One of the items was a helicopter ride off the island. A day at the spa caught my interest. Someone had donated a year membership to a fitness center, someone else a trip for two to Paris.

Kate leaned closer, pointing to the letters on the fifth page. "Look. Here are our names and the photo of the painting we donated."

Kind of boring compared to the other donated items, but it was a large piece, and I'd spent many hours on it.

Kate turned halfway on her chair and waved. "There's Stella and Isaac. Stella looks so pretty."

I'd thought they would sit with us, but they sat with Isaac's friends.

An announcer on the stage stood in front of the podium. He dusted something off his tailored gray suit jacket and grinned. "Good evening, beautiful people. My name is Aaron."

Polite clapping filled the tent.

The speaker took a bow. "Thank you, my friends. And thank you so much for coming. Ian and his crew have been working hard to set up this amazing auction. I'm not going to bore you with a long speech. That's Ian's job."

Laughter rang in the air.

"So, without further ado, let's give a hand to the marvelous, handsome Ian Bordonaro."

The thundering applause faded as Ian strutted across the stage from the side. He had been waiting to be announced. I had been so focused on Aaron, I hadn't seen Ian.

My breath hitched, and my heart skipped a beat. He sported a fine silver suit, the material hugging his muscular frame. He moved with ease and confidence, commanding the stage.

The men cheered, and the women blew wolf whistles. When he raised his hand to quiet the crowd, his gaze zoned in on me as if he knew exactly where I'd be seated. The sly tug of his lips and his twinkling eyes had me melting. It suddenly got hot despite the cool breeze.

"Good evening, friends," Ian said. "For those of you who don't know me, I'm Ian Bordonaro. We're gathered here for a great cause. Some of you know friends or loved ones suffering from dementia. It's a terrible disease, but with your help, we can fight back—enough of the serious talk. There's a long list of hardworking, dedicated people I want to thank, along with those who donated priceless items for the auction. Their names are listed on our website as well as in the pamphlet. I know you're anxious to get started, so let me introduce you to Rachel Bates."

I'd thought Ian would be busy taking care of business, but he came off the podium and sat in the empty chair beside me. He waved at Lee and Kate, then he gave me the most innocent puppy eyes, his long eyelashes fluttering. Acting boyish and cute.

"Hello, Abby," he said.

A smile played on my lips. "Hello, Ian. Great speech. Are you allowed to sit here? Shouldn't you be up there doing something?"

His shoulder touched mine, his warm breath brushing against my cheek. "But I'd much rather be here with you."

I flushed with warmth and used the auction stick to fan myself. Ian smelled like lavender and the ocean breeze. The scent whisked me back to the night on the beach when the two of us had been alone under the night sky and the stars.

Guilt rebounded through me just as quickly. I shook off the thought as Rachel began her speech and presented the first item. A trip to the Bahamas.

I sat up taller, prepared to give Rachel all my attention, when Ian patted his face.

"I'm not just a face of this auction," Ian whispered. "I'm allowed—"

"Shhh …" I placed a finger over my lips. "We've started."

Ian crossed his arms and frowned, like a child who had been scolded, but I could feel his eyes on me.

He bumped my shoulder lightly. "I just want to say, you look beautiful."

Heat flushed up my neck, and I swallowed to maintain my composure. I couldn't look at him. He was dangerously close, and if I'd turned, our lips would touch.

"Thank you," I said softly. I craned my neck a fraction to see him smirk, those pirate eyes staring back at me. "You look beautiful, too."

I tried to break my shyness by drawing attention back to him. Sitting next to him was too distracting, and the next thing I heard was Rachel saying *sold.*

Rachel held up a large photo. "This isn't something you get in stores. This is a seventy-seven-inch 8k resolution flat screen. It has Dolby vision HDR Support. IQ Enhancement Technology. Built-in Wi-Fi & Ethernet Connectivity. And so much more. Bidding starts at twenty thousand."

Someone from the back raised their bidding stick.

"Thirty grand. Do I hear thirty-one?" Rachel said.

A lady from the second row raised her stick.

"Do I hear thirty-two? Thirty-three. Thirty-four. Thirty-five?

Thirty-five. Going once. Twice. Anyone? Last call. Sold."

"These items are boring," Ian said.

I cocked my eyebrows at him. "Then what would be interesting?"

"That one." He pointed to the stage, his eyes wide with interest.

I smiled when I shifted my attention to Rachel. She was holding my painting of an angel wing seashell on the sand, water rippling around it. I had painted it specifically for this auction.

"It's beautiful," Ian said. "That's worth all my money."

I shook my head, smiling. "Well, I hope you have lots of money, then."

"This beautiful painting is one of a kind," Rachel went on. "Donated by Abby Fuller and Kaitlyn Chang, the owners of Carousel Gallery. It's called *Forever in my Heart*. Bidding starts at ten thousand."

Ian turned his gaze to me. "*Forever in my Heart?* You remembered the myth behind the seashell."

I stared into his deep, dark eyes. "Of course. What you said was beautiful."

When Ian had told me the story of the angel diving into the ocean because he couldn't be with the woman he loved, I'd put away the waterfall painting I had planned to donate for the auction and painted this one.

"Twenty thousand," Rachel said.

Staring intently at Ian, I hadn't heard Rachel call the other numbers. Surely, she hadn't gone from ten to twenty. Then the bid went up to thirty.

"Going once. Twice … Thirty thousand, anyone?"

Ian raised his stick.

Kate and Lee gawked at him.

"What are you doing?" I whispered harshly. "I can paint you another one."

"I don't want the second one. I want this one. This is an original."

The bid went up again.

"Forty," Rachel said. "We got forty."

I looked over my shoulder to see who Ian was bidding against, but I couldn't see the person. This was for a great cause, but I didn't want Ian spending a lot of money on a painting I could easily duplicate.

Then, at last, Rachel said, "Fifty?"

Ian raised his stick.

"Fifty-two? Fifty going once. Twice. Sold to Ian Bordonaro."

Chapter Twenty~Seven — Declaration

I covered my face, trying not to hyperventilate. Ian just spent fifty grand on a painting he could have easily purchased for five. Again, I reminded myself that he was doing it for the charity, and he would have donated that much, anyway.

The auction continued for another hour. We gathered to the other side where the tables were already set, and dinner was served.

As the sun lowered, the soft moonlight and the bright stars graced the night. White lights snaked around the palm trees, and electric candles on the table brightened the surrounding area.

"So, where are you going to put that statue of the mask?" I asked Lee and Kate.

"In our bedroom," Lee said.

"In our bedroom?" Kate laughed.

Ian set down his wine glass after taking a drink. "Lee likes to collect weird things and put them in his bedroom. You should already know that about him, Kate."

We shared a laugh.

Lee and Ian informed us which family owned what businesses as we continued our meal. Who'd gotten married or divorced. Who had slept with whom. A real-life soap opera.

Kate rolled her eyes suddenly and mumbled something in my ear, but I missed what she said. Then someone tapped my shoulder. I knew who it was by Kate's expression before I had turned.

"Oh, hi. Je—"

Jessica didn't let me finish. As always, she cut to the chase.

"Lee. Ian." She wiggled her fingers, batting her eyelashes.

Jessica skipped over my sister and ignored the other couple at our table. I'd wished Stella and Isaac sat with us, but they were at another table with Isaacs's friends.

"Jessica." Ian flashed a quick grin.

Lee gave her a curt nod.

Jessica let out a soft sound, something like a clearing of her throat, and placed a hand on Ian's arm. "Anyway, congratulations on your painting, Ian. It's beautiful. I'll be shopping for art soon to fill up the wall space at my new home." She turned to me. "It's too bad Tyler won't be able to attend the father and son event. I'm so sorry about that."

She sounded genuine, but I never knew, when it came to that woman. Yes, she was nice to me, but occasionally she said the most insensitive things, bordering on rude. I thought she was trying sometimes, but had a serious lack of people skills and didn't know how to communicate with any subtlety. Either that or I was reading her wrong, and she had zero redeeming qualities.

"Tyler is going," Ian said matter-of-factly. "I'm taking him."

"You're his father?" Jessica glanced between Ian and me, then she shook her head. "Oh, silly me. I'm not thinking straight. I had a bit much to drink. Tyler's father is … you know …" She lowered her voice. "Dead. You're being nice to take him. That's so sweet of you, Ian. You're so kind to people who need help. Thanks for coming to my rescue." Jessica rubbed his arm again. "Anyway, I better get back to my table. Ian, don't forget to save me a dance."

I peered up to the stars and began to count the nearest ones. I needed something to distract myself from jumping on top of that woman. Never in my entire life had I wanted to punch someone so badly. I also needed to get rid of the jealously brewing inside me.

Ian could be friends with or date any women. He also had the right to rescue anyone. Apparently, that's what he did—rescued women. Perhaps I wanted to be the only one.

Ugh! Stop these nonsense thoughts.

"That's so sweet of you to take Tyler, Ian," Kate said. "Thank you. Abby didn't tell me." She glared at me with a we're-going-to-talk-about-this-later look.

I hadn't told my sister because I didn't want to get a lecture from her or have to explain anything. Besides, we'd been busy, and the topic never came up.

Kate wiped her mouth with the white fabric napkin and set it back on her lap. "What was that all about with Jessica, Ian?"

Leave it to my sister to be nosey, but I was glad she had asked.

"Jessica and I are friends," Ian said. "I've known her for years. She had a flat tire the other day, and I happened to be on the same road. I fixed her flat, and the next day she came over to give me a carrot cake to thank me. I invited her in, and we talked for hours. She does better one on one."

What else did she do for you? Stop. Stop. Stop.

"I bet she does." Lee raised an eyebrow.

Lee's comment didn't help, even though he was kidding. He *was* kidding, right?

After dinner was over and dessert was served, upbeat music wafted out into the night from giant speakers. Some people gathered in groups to chat while the others danced.

Ian excused himself to take a phone call, and Kate and Lee were talking to Lee's friends. As I sat there deciding whether to go home, I realized I hadn't driven, and I would have to call a cab. I didn't want Kate and Lee to leave early on my account.

As I contemplated what to do, I people watched. I used to be confident, bolder, and made conversation easily, but after Steve passed away, something in me had died. I didn't like this version of me. Where had this shy, timid woman come from?

I spotted Ian walking back to our table, but woman after woman grabbed his attention to talk to him. Some were simply greeting him, a hug and a kiss on the cheek. Others clutched his hands as if they didn't want to let him go.

He was on the move again, but this time Jessica stopped him. She was so naturally flirty with him. The way she smiled, the way she caressed his shoulders. And, to my horror, he seemed to be enjoying her company. Then she dragged him to the dancing area.

The music was loud and bouncy, and Ian occasionally put his hand on her hip as they danced. To make things worse, Stella and Isaac joined them. I needed to look away. What was I doing, spying on them?

I went farther out toward the cliff, toward the ocean, to be alone in my thoughts and lose myself in this splendid view. The strong wind pushed me back, so I wrapped my arms to keep me warm and steady.

Would I be that widow who never moved forward, never found love again? I couldn't imagine my life with anyone else besides Steve. I didn't belong here. I didn't want to be here. Why had I agreed to go in the first place?

As these thoughts circulated through my mind, I decided to call for a ride and let Kate know I was leaving. But then something warm draped over my shoulders. Ian had taken off his suit jacket and placed it over me.

"If you stand here too long, you might fly away. Then I'll have to jump to catch you. That might be a little bit hard to do. Although, I could cross that off on the dangerous side of my bucket list, if I survive."

I snorted. "Thank you." I tugged his jacket tighter.

"Were you thinking of painting this view? I hope so. I would buy it in a heartbeat."

"I think I will." A lie, sort of. Now that he'd mentioned it, I thought, *why not.* "And you're not buying anything from me. I owe you a painting for everything you've done and will do."

I took a step back from the force of the wind, my hair slapping my face. He grabbed my arms, thinking I might trip, but we both ended up stumbling from the slope of the hill. My back thumped on the fence, Ian blocking my view of the party.

I swallowed a nervous lump. His eyes held a familiar intensity.

"I want to do more, Abby," he said.

"You don't need to do more, Ian. You've done plenty."

He cleared his throat, his attention on the grass, then back to me. "I knew the day I met you that I would love you. I think you feel something for me, too, but your grief or guilt is holding you back. We can take it slow. I want to spend as many days with you as you're willing to give me."

"Ian ... I ..." I began, but he continued.

"You know I've dated many women, but I never felt this kind of strong connection with them. I lived day to day, even being reckless at times, but after my mother passed away, something changed in me." He clutched his chest. "I realized that though I have many years ahead of me, I want them to be meaningful. I want them to be meaningful with you. Let me mend your broken heart. I want to give you and Tyler the world."

He lowered his eyes to my mouth, caressing my hair away from my face. This man who had become my friend, whom I admired and respected, had a hold on me I didn't want. And, at the same time, I didn't want to let go. The fact that he included my son in his life meant more to me than he could ever know.

I was hypnotized, watching his lips coming closer while his gaze bored into mine as if asking for my permission. *Shiver me timbers.* I might just give in.

"Abby ..." His voice came low and gruff, almost a growl as if fighting the urge to say or do something.

"I really like you—" I needed to say something after his sweet declaration, but perhaps I shouldn't have started with, "I really like you."

Ian's eyes grew darker, and he repeated my name, then crushed his lips to mine. Oh, sweet heavens above. His kiss was soft and tender, growing more intense when I wrapped my arms around his shoulders and pulled him in.

I had forgotten what it felt like to be wanted, desired, and kissed like this. I had forgotten how good it felt. I had forgotten how to kiss, and hoped I was doing it right. But Ian ... with Ian ... it felt so right. Kissing him came easy, our lips and tongues tangling, moving in sync.

When he groaned, I melted into him. He gripped me tighter. He had me spellbound, back to the ocean when it was just the two of us. The ground beneath me crumbled, and my world spun. Dizzy, I was floating to the moon and the stars. The music, the people, my thoughts of leaving the party vanished.

Ian tasted like wine and chocolate, and I wanted more of him, more of his kisses, more of his touches. More of this incredible man.

I moaned, my grip on him growing tighter. I had fought and fought, refused to care about him more than as a friend, but it was too late now. The rush of wanting him broke like a dam. And his kiss undid me. Half torn with pleasure and desire, the other half by guilt and loss. The second half won.

I jerked away, breathless. "Ian ..." I shook my head as tears pooled in my eyes. "I can't. I can't do this."

Ian's fingers grazed my arm, but closed on air when I took another step back. "Abby ..."

I retreated even more, and he squeezed his eyes shut. As my heels sank into the dirt, my steps uneven and tripping on my own feet, I ran, trying to cover my sobbing face.

I needed air. I needed space. What was I doing? I liked Ian a lot, but I wasn't ready to let go of Steve—not just yet.

Chapter Twenty~Eight — Revelation

I texted my sister to let her know I had called a driver and left. Ian might tell Lee, or he would try to forget what had happened between us and move on to the next woman. Maybe even Jessica.

Oh, God. That thought made me nauseous.

No matter. I reminded myself that I wasn't the best for Ian. I couldn't give him all of me, and it wouldn't be fair to him. As soon as I got home, I changed, picked up Tyler from Lee's place, and drove back home.

I had missed calls from Kate and Ian. I'd thought it was best I didn't talk to Ian, so I messaged my sister.

> **Abby: I'm fine. Please don't worry about**
> **me. I'm going to bed. Don't come over.**

I lied, of course, but my sister didn't come over.

The next day, after I dropped off Tyler at school, I went for a run instead of working. I needed to clear my thoughts. I needed to stop thinking about that damn kiss that had ruined me in more ways than one. Jogging wasn't working, so I sprinted as fast as my legs and lungs would allow. That didn't work either.

Ian's face replaced the trees, the cars, the houses, and every which way I turned. Before I knew it, I was standing in front of Izzy's Café.

I walked in, sweating, and looked behind the cash register to spot dark hair peppered with white. Not her daughter.

"Izzy," I chirped, a bit louder than I meant to.

She jerked back and held her hand to her heart, panting. "Goodness, dear. What's gotten into you?"

Just the sight of her made me smile, my worries pushed to the side, even if she sounded a bit annoyed.

"I'm so sorry. It's so good to see you. You weren't here the last time I came." Probably best not to tell her that a part of me had thought she'd died.

She leaned forward, her elbows on the front counter. "I took a couple of weeks off, and I'm so glad I did. So you met my daughter."

"Yes, I did. She's lovely."

"Thank you." She straightened and grabbed a paper mug. "Same latte?"

"Do you even need to ask?" I gave her a sly smirk.

"So …" Izzy got busy making my drink. "I have something to tell you." She paused for good measure, inhaled a deep breath, and said, "I sold the café."

"What? No. Izzy." I frowned, unable to hide my disappointment.

"I'm getting too old, and I'd like to do things before I die, Abby." She snorted and grabbed the soy milk out of the fridge.

I lowered my head. "I understand. When's your last day?"

"End of next month. Jason and I are going to do some traveling. Go visit our grandkids and live life. I've been stuck to this café for so long." She cupped the hand I had rested on the counter, and her expression turned somber. "I'll miss the people. I'll miss you."

I gave her a warm smile as tears pooled in my eyes. "I'm going to miss you, too." More than she would ever know. I not only came here for the delicious lattes, but for the guidance she didn't know she was giving me. Just talking to her made me feel better.

She patted our clasped hands and went behind the machine to whip the latte. "So, how are Tyler and Kate?"

"Kate is engaged."

She beamed a smile. "Oh, that's wonderful. When? How?"

As I gave her details on how Ian and I had helped Lee, a pang stabbed my chest.

Izzy narrowed her eyes behind her glasses. "Did something happen? Who is this Ian? Why haven't you told me about him before?"

I laughed nervously. Izzy knew my life story, and she could read me like a book.

I glanced to the door to see if anyone was coming, then focused back on her. "Ian is Lee's friend. I met him four years ago, but we've become good friends recently."

She gave me a suspicious sidelong glance. "What do you mean by good friend? Men and women can't be friends, especially when both of them are single. But that's just my opinion."

I disagreed, but said nothing. "It's complicated."

She regarded me for a moment and put the lid on my drink. "What does Tyler think of Ian?"

"Ty really likes him. Ian is good with kids, and in fact, Ian volunteered to take Ty to the father and son event at his school."

The words came out too fast, and I realized my mistake when I finished. I shouldn't have said anything. Now she would see right through me. But when I recalled that conversation in the car, it made me smile.

Izzy tugged her lips to the side, hiding behind a smile. "So, Ian is more than a friend. You like him, don't you?"

It sounded like a statement.

"I—I can't. I mean—but he kissed me. I kissed him back. I wanted to. I—"

She dipped her head, then looked up at me. "Abby, I know how you're feeling. I've been there before."

I cocked my head in question. "But—"

She handed me my latte. "I've never told you this, but I've been married twice. My first husband died from a heart attack after ten years of marriage. I was devasted, heartbroken. I cursed the world for making me a single parent to my two girls. To pay the bills, I bought this café. I raised two lovely daughters on my own."

After hearing her story, I admired and respected her even more. I wondered if her daughter got the angel tattoo in honor of her father.

She continued. "A few years later, I met Jason through a friend. He came around often and was even good with my girls. When he wanted more, I told him I wasn't ready. I was fighting guilt and this new love I felt for him. I was scared out of my mind."

I took a hot sip as I pondered her words, my fingers warm around the mug.

"I know how you feel, Abby, but the reason why I'm telling you my story is so that you don't let a good man go. Also, not every man wants to deal with another man's child. If Ian is willing to take Ty to the father-son event, well, I think he's a keeper. We came to Earth to be together and will continue to do so after this life. You will see Steve one day, but for now, you and Tyler need to live life to the fullest."

"Izzy. Thank you so much for sharing your story." I reached over the counter, my arms halfway around her in a squeeze.

Izzy smiled. "I'll always be there for you, Abby. I consider you a part of my family. My 'ohana. Do you know what 'ohana means?"

I hadn't before, not until Kate had told me. Tears pooled in my eyes, I was so humbled by her words and affection toward Tyler and me.

"Yes," I said. "'Ohana means family, and no one gets left behind. Something like that."

She nodded. "Always remember the spirit of 'ohana. Nobody gets left behind or forgotten. That's a quote from *Lilo and Stitch*." Izzy offered an exaggerated smile with all her teeth.

I told Izzy I would visit her soon and left. On my way home, something made me text my sister.

> **Abby: Can you take care of Tyler for me?**
> **I'm going to be gone for a few days.**

The decision had been made, and I had to act on it. I didn't have time to pick up my son. I had to go home and pack. I would make up an excuse and explain to Tyler why I'd told him over the phone.

> **Kate: Sure. Of course. Is everything all right?**

My fingers flew over the letters.

> **Abby: I'm going to Florida to see my**
> **mother-in-law.**

Instead of getting a text back, Kate called me. I told Kate about the kiss Ian and I had shared and how my emotions were conflicted. The only way to resolve my guilt and move on was to visit my mother-in-law in Florida. Thankfully, she didn't think my idea was crazy, and agreed with me wholeheartedly.

Chapter Twenty~Nine — Florida

It might sound strange, but letting my mother-in-law know how I felt about another man would be almost like getting a blessing from Steve that it was okay to move on.

I took the first flight to Florida. Too many memories came crashing in. We had visited his parents the summer before he had proposed to me. I texted Michelle, my sister-in-law, when I got my luggage, and waited for her in the waiting area outside.

"Abby!" Michelle waved.

I ran three cars down and smacked her in the head with my purse as I tried to hug her. It was so good to see her.

"I'm so glad you're here." She hefted my luggage into the trunk as I got into the passenger side.

Michelle pulled into the oncoming traffic and glanced at me over her shoulder. "Mom would have come, but she thought it was best to wait at home."

"That's okay. I understand."

Peggy had developed rheumatoid arthritis after Steve passed away. It could have been a coincidence, but I always wondered if heartache had caused her health problems.

"So, how are ..." That was when I noticed a ring on her finger. "Michelle? When did you get engaged?"

I'd known she was dating a dentist, but I didn't know how serious they were. And if I could be honest with myself, I was a bit hurt that she hadn't called to tell me. We didn't talk as much as we used to, and that might have been my fault, but still, she could have let me know.

Her lips tugged at the corners, and at the sly sidelong glance, she reminded me of Steve. Steve and Michelle didn't look like siblings, but sometimes their expressions reminded me of each other. Steve looked like their father; Michelle, their mother. The only feature they shared was the pretty green eyes.

She wiggled her fingers at me, and her two-carat diamond sparkled in the sunlight. "Garret proposed to me last weekend. I was going to call you, but then you messaged me, so I decided to surprise you instead."

"I'm so happy for you. Do you have a date set?"

Michelle checked her mirrors and changed lanes. "Not yet, but I'll let you know when I do. I want Tyler to be the ring bearer, if that's okay."

"Of course. He would love that. In fact, my sister got engaged, too, and Tyler is going to be their ring bearer."

"Perfect. Congrats to Kate."

During the drive through heavy traffic to Peggy's house, Michelle and I talked about work, our parents, and Tyler. When we arrived, my mother-in-law had the door wide open, waving at us as we pulled into the driveway.

Peggy lived in a two-story house with a tidy, trimmed front yard. Rose bushes lined the walkway to the door. I slammed the car door behind me and rushed up to her.

Peggy used to care about the white showing in her hair, but she had let it grow. The wrinkles on her forehead and around the eyes had deepened. Michelle and Peggy had been through so much—first Steve and then my father-in-law's death shortly after.

"Abby. Welcome." Her voice cracked. "It's so good to see you."

While Michelle brought in my bag, Peggy gave me the tightest hug, and we shared happy and sad tears. After settling into the family room, Michelle served iced tea and sat next to me on the sofa.

I glanced around the room to see if there was anything new from the last time Tyler and I had visited. Besides the addition of a simple wooden cabinet and a couple of paintings I had gifted them hanging in her living room, all was the same.

"You haven't aged, Abby," Peggy said.

I placed my glass down on the table. "Thank you."

Peggy leaned back into the sofa and rested her hands on her lap. "How's my Tyler?"

She curled her fingers inward, rubbing the tell-tale knobs of her arthritis. Peggy's condition had worsened. I would ask Michelle about her situation later. She might not want to talk about it, and I didn't want to spring it on her.

"Ty is perfect." My smile widened. "He's doing well in school. We plan to start piano lessons in the summer, and also baseball."

Peggy smiled, but it didn't reach her eyes. Only sadness showed in them. "Steve liked baseball." Her voice was soft and weak.

Steve had played first base in high school. The Dodgers were his favorite team, and he had taken me to games at Dodger Stadium whenever we had the chance. We'd spent many summer evenings watching games at home with our friends.

Peggy and I talked and laughed, reminiscing and discussing Michelle's wedding plans. When the sun dipped lower, we went out to dinner and came home. I'd told them I wanted to visit Steve at his gravesite tomorrow alone. They'd understood.

Instead of sleeping in the guest room, I went upstairs to Steve's childhood bedroom. I had seen his room when we'd visited before, but the last time I'd been there, I couldn't face the room alone.

Nothing had changed. The baseball trophies and academic achievement plaques he'd gotten in high school lined the bookcase. He had a few books on the shelves, but none looked well-worn. Steve hadn't been a reader.

Steve had told me he wanted to play professional baseball, but he'd thought he wouldn't make the cut, so he'd decided to major in business. He was glad he had, or he wouldn't have met me.

I brushed a finger over his senior portrait on the desk, and tears prickled my eyes. Steve had been a good man. He hadn't deserved cancer. He'd deserved a longer life. I tucked myself inside the blanket and called Kate to speak to my son.

Chapter Thirty — Confession

The driver I had hired for the day took me past the mall Steve and I had shopped at and restaurants where we'd eaten together. My heart knotted painfully at the memories. They seemed like they'd happened yesterday, and yet so long ago.

I tried not to tear up as I people watched. Citizens crossing the streets, families of tourists taking pictures, residents going in and out of their apartments. It was good to see such busy lives, like the life I'd once had. After Steve had died, I'd needed a slower pace.

Steve had been originally buried in New York, but his parents had moved his body when I moved to Kauai. Last Christmas, when I'd brought Tyler to see his grandmother, I had visited Steve at the burial site.

I could talk to Steve back at home, and I often did, but I felt closer to him here in Florida. If I spoke to him here, maybe I would know what to do.

The driver dropped me off at the cemetery and waited. I purchased a bouquet of flowers at the small flower shop. My nerves were all over the place as I walked the path toward Steve's plot.

I kneeled and placed the bouquet inside the pot. I sat on the grass and leaned against the tombstone, inhaling a deep breath and exhaling a longer one.

I took a moment of this quiet peace to settle my nerves and my hammering heart. It had been a while since I'd had a few days to myself. I could sit there all day to recharge and face the world again.

A few families came and went, but what broke me was seeing a little girl with her mom. They laid a bouquet of flowers next to a tombstone. The little girl reminded me of Tyler, close to the age he'd been when Steve died.

So many broken hearts here. So much sadness. And then I felt my own tears pool.

I had no speech planned, so I didn't know where to begin. Perhaps I should start with a greeting.

"Hello, Steve," I said softly, then my voice cracked. "You're probably wondering why I'm here when I could be talking to you back home. I had to come. I have something to tell you."

Tears streamed down my face as guilt-wracked my soul. *How do I tell him I might be in love with someone else? How can I do this to him?*

I wiped my eyes. Getting to the point might make things easier. "I met someone. His name is Ian Bordonaro." I smiled when I said his name. "Ian is one of Lee's good friends, and that's how I met him. He's intelligent and has a big heart. He's good to Ty, and Ty likes him, too. He offered to take our son to a school father and son event, since you …" I swallowed to dislodge the twist of pain in my chest and the lump in my throat.

"Anyway, I came here to get your permission to … I know you want me to move on with my life with someone else eventually, but I don't know if I'm ready. Ian told me he would take things slow. I guess that's a sign that I'm worth the wait and that he's worth taking a chance on. I don't know what I'm doing. I only know that I miss you so much. I can't … This is too hard. We were supposed to have a life together."

I curled my knees up to my chest and leaned my head against the cold stone, as if I could lean my head against his shoulder. Tears streamed down my face, and I paused to collect myself.

"Whatever happens, whomever I date, I promise that Ty and I will never forget you. No matter how many years pass, you'll always be in our hearts and in our memories."

I wiped my tears again and ran my knuckles under my nose, sniffling.

"As silly as it sounds, I wish you could give me a sign that you're okay with me dating, but …" I released a long sigh. "Of course, you can't, and …"

I'd thought I would feel better if I spoke to Steve at his burial site, but I didn't. In fact, I felt worse. I pushed my palms to my face, wondering what on earth I was doing, and then I went back to Peggy's house.

After dinner, we sat on the back patio in the outdoor chairs. The humid Florida night settled over me, and the darkness filled with chirruping insects.

Peggy peered up at the night sky. "I love coming out here to look at the stars. On a clear night like tonight, you can see the Milky Way. Steve loved the stars, too. When he was little, he told me that he'd become a star and be the brightest one day. Sometimes, I'll look for the brightest one and pretend that it's Steve looking down at me, saying, 'See, Mom, I told you I would be a star.'" She snorted to hold in her sob. "No parent should have to see their child leave the world before they do. No one." She cleared her throat and looked at me. "I'm sorry. I'm rambling. But seeing you makes me miss my son more."

"I'm sorry," I said softly.

"No, don't be." Peggy dabbed her eyes with her knuckle. "You two were a pair. He loved you very much, Abby. You and Tyler were his world. He was so excited when he found out he was going to be a father."

I wiped my tears, recalling how nervous I'd been, to tell him. I'd thought he would be upset. I was still in college, and he'd been in grad school. Getting pregnant had sped up our plans. Perhaps things happen for a reason, the right place, and the right time.

If I hadn't gotten pregnant, then we would have waited. Steve would have gotten sick after we moved to New York, and we wouldn't have tried to have children. Tyler would never have been born.

Michelle, who had been quiet, said, "Not to rush you, Abby, but how long did you plan on staying?"

"I leave tomorrow afternoon."

"Tomorrow. That's so soon." Peggy frowned. "But I'm guessing that since you didn't bring Tyler, you came here for business?"

I brushed a strand away from my face and cleared my throat. "This might seem silly, but I came to get your blessing."

They both cocked their eyebrows.

I rubbed my hands together, feeling awkward. I should have done this over the phone. No. It was better in person. I needed closure, reassurance, or some sign. Something to make me feel less guilty, or I might never move forward.

"For what, Abby?" Peggy sounded concerned.

Here goes nothing. Just say it.

I bit my bottom lip and glanced between my mother-in-law and Michelle, wondering if they would feel betrayed or that I had let them down. That I hadn't mourned Steve long enough.

"I met someone." The words made my heart thump faster. "Nothing has happened. He wants more than friendship." Then the tightness in my chest eased to have confessed openly.

"What do you want?" Michelle said.

There was no accusation in her tone, but I wasn't sure how she truly felt.

I lowered my head, then raised my chin. "I don't know. I'm not ready to jump into a relationship, but I'm open to dating and taking things slow."

"So, this is why you came," Peggy said, her tone neutral.

"Yes. You two mean so much to me, and I didn't want to do it over the phone." I shuddered a breath. "I will always love Steve. Ty and I will never forget him. I don't know what the future will hold, and I don't know if I'll ever find love again, but I want you to know that no matter what, you're my family."

My mother-in-law's features crinkled, and she clutched her chest as tears streamed down her face. "I knew this day would come, but I didn't know I was going to react this way. Sorry." Her lips pinched together. "Of course, you have our blessing, Abby. You're still young, and you have another season of life ahead of you. It'll be good for Tyler to have another role model besides you." She blinked and blinked. "Just don't forget us, okay?"

"Oh, Peggy." I rushed over and wrapped her in my arms, relieved but also overwhelmed. "I promise."

"I need a hug, too," Michelle sniffed.

Peggy and I broke apart, smiling, and then I hugged Michelle.

"Well, whoever this guy is, he'll be lucky to have you and Tyler in his life," Michelle said.

"Thank you." I shrugged. "I don't know if anything will happen between us. I kind of left him hanging."

"You did?" Michelle's eyes rounded. "If he cares for you, he'll give you time. You'll have to send me a picture of him." Michelle lightened the oppressive mood, but she cut it short. "I'll be right back. I have something to give you."

As I waited for Michelle, I sat next to Peggy again. It felt good to get to talk to them, but there was still something lingering inside that I couldn't let go.

The screen door opening halted our conversation, and Michelle stepped out with a white envelope and a wrapped box. The shape and size of the envelope looked like it could be a holiday card. Michelle remained standing and held out the items to me.

"This is for you, Abby."

"For me?" I rose and took them graciously. "Why?"

Michelle shifted, somewhat nervous. "It's not from me. It's from Steve. He asked me to give it to you when I thought you needed it. I think you coming here is a sign that you do. I hope it gives you comfort." She peered down at her mother and offered a hand.

I waited until they were both inside and ripped open the seal with trembling fingers.

Chapter Thirty~One — The Letter

My stomach somersaulted—and then some—from the anticipation of what I'd find in Steve's letter. I wished Michelle had given it to me when Steve passed away, but I couldn't be upset with her. She was only fulfilling Steve's wishes.

I didn't know if my heart had any more room for pain, because whatever was in that letter was going to break me to pieces. With my trembling hands, pulse racing, I unfolded the paper.

> My dearest Abby,
>
> If you're reading this letter, I'm no longer in this life with you and our son. I asked Michelle to give you this letter when she thought you needed it the most. I don't know when that time will be, but a selfish part of me wishes you never will.
>
> I hate that I won't be there for you. I hate that I won't be able to teach Ty how to ride a bike or play baseball. I hate that I'm dying, and there's not a damn thing I can do. And most of all, I hate that I have to make you a widow.
>
> I'm so sorry, Abby. Please forgive me. I'd give anything not to cause you this pain. This is not the life you deserve. I wish I could change fate, but this only means that I'm not supposed to be yours forever.
>
> With that being said, I want you to know that whenever you're ready to move on without me,

you have my blessing. I know you. Guilt will split you in half. Be free of guilt, sweetheart. Be free to love someone else, but don't forget me and the good times we shared. Life is too short. You and I know this firsthand, now. Live your life to the fullest. Make memories.

I love you, sweetheart. I love you more than you will ever know, which is the reason why I want you to move on without me. The only thing I ask is that you place the gift I'm giving you wherever you want to remember me. To remember how much I loved you and how much I want you and Tyler to be happy.

There's a story about an angel who loved a human so much that he wanted to be a human. When he was refused, he dove into the ocean because he couldn't bear the pain of losing her. When his wings touched the water, thousands of his feathers turned into seashells that looked like angel wings. These seashells are rare, and somehow they find grieving people who have lost their loved ones. It's a reminder that love never dies, even when the person is gone.

I am that angel who wants to be with you, but can't. But I am with you always. I will always be grateful for your love. Grateful that you gave me a son. And even though our time was short, those were the best years of my life.

If there ever was such a thing as soulmates, you were mine, and I was yours. But sometimes even soulmates don't get their happy-ever-after. I was your first love, but someone will be your last. He's one damn lucky guy.

We came to earth to be together and will continue to do so after this life.

I love you across the galaxies and beyond,

Steve

My body trembled, my chest heaved, and tears came faster than I could wipe them. This letter punctured a hole in my chest, and at the same time, healed it. I hugged his letter as if I could hug him and sobbed and sobbed, riding the wave of my pain.

After no more tears were shed, I opened the box and took out a dove-white seashell as big as my palm. Two angel wing seashells were aligned to create a heart.

Steve couldn't have left me a more perfect gift.

Sometimes fate was kind.

Chapter Thirty-Two — A New Beginning

Receiving my mother-in-law's blessing had given me some solace, but Steve's letter had given me the peace I needed.

Family was important to me, and even though Steve was gone, Peggy and Michelle were still my family. I would always care about them and be there for them. And I wanted Tyler to have a relationship with them, no matter the distance.

It was hard saying goodbye to Peggy and Michelle. We hugged and shed tears, and I promised to bring Tyler during our next visit. When Michelle dropped me off at the airport, I'd told her I would keep in touch.

While I waited at the gate, I sent a text message to Kate, letting her know I was at the airport. Then I sent a message to Ian as my pulse raced, asking him to call me. I had so much to say to him. I had run out on him, then ignored him.

I stared at the phone screen—no answer from Ian. Not to worry. He must be busy and would get back to me.

Tapping my feet like a drum, I continued to stare at the screen. I apologized to the older woman beside me when she cleared her throat. I shifted in my seat and glanced at people walking by. The sound of rolling suitcases and the children running in circles behind me faded when my phone dinged. Excitement coursed through my veins. I clicked on it and felt disappointed. It was from my sister.

> **Kate:** Got your message. See you at home. Have a safe flight.

> **Abby:** Do you know where Ian is? I can't get ahold of him.

I knew that message was silly. Kate didn't know Ian's schedule, but I felt desperate to ask someone.

> **Kate:** Did you try calling?

I realized I needed to see him in person. There was too much to say. When I didn't answer, dots scrolled in.

Kate: You're being weird.

Abby: If you see Ian, tell him to check his phone. Also, tell Lee to tell him.

I didn't know where this aggressive side of me was coming from, but Ian had always texted me back soon after. He was probably busy. He had a life. But what if he was with another woman? What if I had blown my chance?

A text came from my sister.

Kate: Lee told me Ian has a business trip planned to Europe.

No. He couldn't leave without hearing what I needed to tell him. I puffed out air as I looked at the time. There was nothing I could do but get home.

When we landed, I immediately turned on my phone and waited … and waited. *Please. Please. Message me back. Tell me you didn't leave town.*

A message from Ian.

Ian: Listen to your voicemail.

That didn't sound like good news. While we waited for the plane to dock at the gate, I clicked the play button and pressed the phone to my ear.

"Abby. I'm so sorry if I've done anything to offend you. I'm also sorry if I've made you feel uncomfortable, but I needed to tell you how I felt before leaving. I had planned a business trip to London, and I'm not sure when I'll be back. Lee will take my place and will take Tyler to the father and son event. I hope you can forgive me and we can be friends. Perhaps the time apart will do us good. Next time you see me, I promise I'll be a good friend you'll be proud to have."

Tyler was going to be disappointed that Lee was taking him instead.

My heart sank to my stomach. Everything I wanted to tell Ian circled into a drain that sucked me under. I couldn't believe he was gone. I hadn't gotten a chance to tell him how I felt. And when he came back, he might not feel the same way about me.

How long was he going to be gone? I couldn't remember what he'd said, or if he even said it at all. I needed more information, and the only person who might know anything was my sister.

As I filed in line to get out of the plane, I called Kate.

"Kate, it's me."

"You landed."

"Yes. Do you know if Ian left already? I need to tell him how I feel about him."

"What?" She sounded surprised. "When did this happen? Who are you? Are you my sister?"

"Stop fooling around. Where is he?" I didn't mean to sound harsh, but I was desperate.

"Geez, Abby. Okay. Like I said in the text, I think he's already gone. I'm so sorry. Wait? Should I be sorry? What did you want to tell him?"

"That I ..." I lowered my voice even though I was walking fast to get to the baggage claim. "Never mind. I'll talk to you later. I gotta get my bag. I'll see you when I pick up Ty."

After I had grabbed my suitcase, I rushed to the taxi line. As the taxi driver drove me home, I messaged Ian, deleted the message, then wrote something, only to delete it again. I repeated this pattern until I finally left him a voice message.

"Ian, I want you to know that you did nothing wrong. You've been a perfect gentleman. I'm sorry I left abruptly without an explanation, but I needed to clear my head and get some closure. There are many things I want to tell you, but I think it's best I tell you in person. I don't know when I'll see you or talk to you, so please be safe. I hope you come back soon. I miss you."

Had I lost my chance with Ian? Had I scared him off? Was he ever coming back? Now that I'd finally admitted to myself how I felt, I wanted to be with him more than anything.

Would I have the courage to speak my mind if Ian called back? I didn't know how to do this. But if Ian didn't care to call, then we weren't meant to be. And I would have to face the fact that I'd blown something that could have been great.

The taxi driver dropped me off at home. I put the toiletries and clothes away from my luggage and placed Steve's gift on my bedside table. I changed into jeans and a T-shirt to pick up my son. I couldn't wait to see him.

I grabbed my car keys and checked my phone one last time. No message from Ian. We hadn't even dated, yet my feelings for him seemed to grow in his absence.

The doorbell rang. I swung around, and it dawned on me that it was Friday. I had forgotten to open the back gate for the gardener, and had forgotten to ask Kate to unlock it. I doubled back to the front door.

"I'm so sorry. I forgot to …" When I got a clear view of the man standing before me, I wondered if I had dreamed him up.

Ian's lips quirked into that devilish smirk and then tugged into a broad grin. "Did you mean it when you said you missed me, on that voicemail?"

I was unable to hide my smile. I was over the moon happy to see him. Backing away, I gave him space to enter.

I shrugged, holding up my thumb and index finger, a small space between the gap. "Maybe just a little bit." I shoved both hands inside my back pocket and took a few steps back. "I thought you were out of town."

Ian closed the door behind him and stepped closer. "I was on my way to the airport, but when I heard 'I hope you come back soon. I miss you,' well, those were magical words." His playfulness was replaced by something serious. "Words I would give anything to hear. Did you mean it, Abby?"

"You were on your way to the airport, but you came here instead?" He had dropped everything for me. And to think I had almost let him slip away.

"Business can wait, but you can't. When you ran away from me at the party, I thought I'd lost you." His face was drawn and pale, a look of hurt flashing in those gorgeous eyes. "If I came here with the wrong impression, I'm sorry. And if you just want to be friends, I'll accept that. I didn't like how we parted ways. Just tell me what you want, Abby, and it's yours."

I swallowed. Yes, I wanted to be more than friends with Ian, but it didn't mean that saying those words were going to be easy. Worse, I didn't know where to start.

"I want to explain something first," I said.

"Let's sit down." He held my hand and led me to the sofa.

I intertwined my fingers on my lap. "What I feel for you is more than friends. But the guilt of moving on broke me. So, I went to see my mother-in-law in Florida." When I told him about Steve's letter, I choked up, and tears welled in my eyes. "What I'm trying to say is that I really like you, Ian. But I need to take things slow, and I need for Tyler to be okay with us."

Ian wiped my tears and grabbed my hands, his warmth penetrating through. "I've already confessed how I feel about you, so you know where I stand. I will do what you ask. I'm going to leave it up to you to pave the path of our relationship. Does that sound good?"

"Yes." I smiled. "I can't believe you're here. When I couldn't get ahold of you, I didn't know if—"

"I'm here, Abby. And, to be honest, I planned the business trip without thinking straight. My thoughts were all over the place, and I was kind of a mess, but I knew we could at least be friends. But when you left that message, I sped here as fast as I could."

I laughed lightly. "You're wonderful, Ian."

"People tell me that all that time." He smirked. "So, how about we pick up Ty together and go out to dinner—just the three of us."

"That sounds like a plan." I rose and faced him, my gaze locking with his. "Thank you for being so patient, and thank you for being good to Ty."

His eyes darkened, and he kissed the back of my hand. "I would wait a lifetime for you, Abby Fuller. My heart was an empty sky, but you gave me the moon and the stars. Steve was your first, but I want to be your last."

Ian knew the right words to say, but I also knew he meant it. Steve was my first, but I knew that Ian would be my last, to the depths of my heart.

Chapter Thirty-Three — Two Weeks Later

"Oh, my goodness. You two look adorable," Kate said as she kept her camera on Ian and Tyler, snapping away.

Ian and Tyler wore the jeans and matching T-shirts I had ordered for them. They read, *Best friends*. Because they were. Ever since Tyler found out Ian and I were dating, Ian had treated Tyler like his own and picked him up after school every day for the past two weeks. Ian worked from home, so he could make his own schedule.

Ian moved to his beach house permanently and wanted Tyler and me to move in with him when I was ready. I didn't know when that would be, but we had time.

"Let me know when the event is over," I said.

Ian looked at the tickets I had handed to him. "We should be done by eight. Then we're going to hit the bars."

Kate snorted, and I shook my head with my lips pursed.

"The bar?" Tyler arched his eyebrows, then he got the joke. "Ohhhh."

"Well, we better get going. Come on, Ty. Let's do this." Ian draped his arm around Tyler, guiding him to the door.

Ian had often taken Tyler to miniature golf after school. He wanted Tyler to get used to the course and feel confident to have fun. Sometimes when I had to work late, Ian would bring me dinner and stay with Tyler until I came home.

"One more picture," Kate said.

Ian and Tyler turned and faced the camera, smiling. I teared up a bit, grateful for Ian. He'd come into my life unexpectedly, and had given us so much joy.

"No more, Auntie Kate." Tyler frowned.

Kate lowered her camera.

Ian snaked his arm around my waist and pulled me closer. "Have fun hanging out with your sister, but save some energy for me." He gave me a quick kiss on the lips, but it traveled all over my body.

While Ian and Tyler played miniature golf, Kate and I planned to organize her wedding itinerary. Lee, Bridget, Stella, and Isaac were coming over soon.

"Hurry home," I whispered in his ear, and lightly bit his earlobe.

"Shiver me timbers." Ian waggled his eyebrows and opened the door.

My sexy pirate.

Tyler kissed my cheek and walked out with Ian.

"I'm so happy for you." Kate rested her head against my shoulder as we watched my boys ease down the driveway.

Kate went to the kitchen to get a drink, and I went to my bedroom to pick up the laundry basket. I passed my bed on my way out, but turned back to the bedside table where I had set Steve's gift.

I brushed my hand over the smooth angel wing seashell and said, "Tyler and I are going to be fine, Steve. Thank you for sending a wonderful man our way. I'll always love you across the galaxies and beyond."

I was ready to live. Ready to make new memories and ready to move on. But Steve would always be in my heart. Love never dies.

We came to earth to be together and will continue to do so after this life. It is the spirit of 'ohana.

About the Author

Mary Ting is an international bestselling, award-winning author. Her books span a wide range of genres, and her storytelling talents have earned a devoted legion of fans, as well as garnered critical praise.

Becoming an author happened by chance. It was a way to grieve the death of her beloved grandmother, and inspired by a dream she had in high school. After realizing she wanted to become a full-time author, Mary retired from teaching after twenty years. She also had the privilege of touring with the Magic Johnson Foundation to promote literacy and her children's chapter book: *No Bullies Allowed.*

www.AuthorMaryTing.com